The Neologist

On the Edge of Droxis

S ETH A. G ROSSMAN

∾ INFINITY
PUBLISHING

ISBN 978-1-4958-0527-1
ISBN 978-1-4958-0543-1 eBook
Library of Congress Catalog Card Number: 0000-0000

Published March 2015

References:

Browning, Robert & Elizabeth B. Browning, 1909, "Any Wife to Any Husband", Love Songs from Robert and Elizabeth Barrett Browning, Rand McNalley & Co., Chicago, IL & New York, NY

Joyce, James, 1934, Ulysses, Random House, First Modern library Edition, NY, NY

Lewis, Noah, 1929, "Going to Germany', music and lyrics, Cannon's Jug Stompers, Victor, V38585 Camden, NJ

Yeats, William Butler, 1933, A Dialogue of Self & Soul, The Winding Stair and Other Poems, Macmillan Publishing Company, NY, NY

INFINITY PUBLISHING
1094 New DeHaven Street, Suite 100
West Conshohocken, PA 19428-2713
Toll-free (877) BUY BOOK
Local Phone (610) 941-9999
Fax (610) 941-9959
Info@buybooksontheweb.com
www.buybooksontheweb.com

The Neologist

On the Edge of Droxis

S<small>ETH</small> A. G<small>ROSSMAN</small>

For Emmanuella

I am content to follow to its source
Every event in action or in thought;
Measure the lot; forgive myself the lot!
When such as I cast out remorse
So great a sweetness flows into the breast
We must laugh and we must sing,
We are blest by every thing,
Every thing we look upon is blest.

William Butler Yeats, 1933
A Dialogue of Self & Soul,
The Winding Stair and Other Poems

With special thanks to: Marina Harrison, Lydia Burdick, Joel Proper, Marcos Bravo, Rev. Truman Goines, Shirley Conway, Jerry Glock, Morton and Sally Grossman, Patricia Sonne, and The Committee.

CONTENTS

PROLOGUE

There is an abundance of you

Swelling broad and deep
behind complaint
banging out against
a strained and tired lament
bent and shard-shook
shaken thought and
justifying think rip

there is a real lip
brushed closely by your ear
there is a light-felt bird
held before the mind
that is as large and
lightly lording, and
lifting full of unknown present
as chaotic
and as broad and deep
as love

Before the mind a bird is floating
a simple chance in pop-filled wildness
that draws the bold

and shameless look
the waiting naked
stripped-to-body nude
and full of flesh
and full of hold and sex and wonder, and
eye in immediate eye of self
and mouthy wet-joy
beat and squirm
and pressing sex joy

A bird before the mind
a thigh in hand
arms wrapped tightly
waists held tight
and bellies touching
abundant in anticipating wonder

wonder that is step-by-step
a walk
a walking bird before the mind

Before us
bird walks
before us is bird

a moment
before the mind

Rev. Truman Goines, 1995

AN AUSPICIOUS OCCASION

It was 1998. Broadway was a stretch of happenings on Manhattan's Upper Westside – perched on the arch of a hill, teased by shadows and light that flickered off the Hudson River. A purposeful grasp of measured and hopeful ambition, curved and tailored, bosomed and plunged with the nip of mountain air swept south along that river's holy call, and mimicked along the avenue. Jack completed his morning Tai Chi, seventeen floors up on the apartment building's roof. He tightened his loose grey sweat pants and slowly walked downstairs to his fifteenth floor apartment for a cup of joe, and later inserted the needle to postpone a diabetic coma.

Inside, the dust mote biographical sit of silence was on the windowsill. "Dust shit backlit with the urbanized crud of mid-autumn morning glare," murmured Jack Neti. He thought about it while sitting in his bathrobe of many colors, psychedelic '60s swirls, smoking an acrid filterless Camel cigarette. He yirkeled towards the small piano and played a blues. The filtered crudup built as sunlight tumbled into more quiet and degenerate

wishes for more auspicious occasions of realized
and shared nakedness. And when the wish would
be granted and desire satisfied and surrendered,
full annihilation would seep in everywhere,
creating molasses ooze rooted in the purest fields
of consciousness ... causing morphogenic filigree
in a banana soup of desire, poetry, and other forms
of erotic blither. Jack was 43 years old, an ex-
government community development bureaucrat,
ex-jazz blues singer, ex-dharma bum, ex-fugitive
of middle-class Amerika, and full-time pilgrim.
"Dem's were de' days," Mugs Durante had
murmured as he took a pee at the local Applebees.
That didn't seem to fit," Jack thought, "but it does."

Jack Neti stared out his window to the West
End Avenue below. The mid-autumn of early
November had an unusually bright sunlight
accompanied by a cool breeze. His thoughts
ranged from descriptions of what he saw: jazzing
poems, conversations overheard on the street,
ideas that floated through his mind, voices and
conversations with others who weren't there,
empathic revelations, and telepathic messages.
After years of working in various corporations
providing sales and management training, Jack
had started his own consulting business based
on his 20-odd years in community development.
This change came about five months ago, about
the time of his 43rd birthday after a visit to a friend
in Popham Beach, Maine. It turned into less of a
regular visit and became a week that changed his

life. His old friend, Truman Goines, a shamanic intermittent social dropout, a best friend whom he'd met in college in 1973, offered to guide him on a shamanic journey. And the funny thing was, it actually was exactly that. Be careful what you wish for.

Jack agreed to go with him, and as he looked back, he put a lot of faith in Truman. But why not? His wife had become interested in another man, which in itself was not a shock. It's just that once again, you have to be careful what you wish for. Jack had wished that they would revisit the premise of the relationship, and they did. In Manhattan, the opportunity for self-examination was endless; and while in one of a slew of self-improvement workshops, Jack saw the inevitable boundaries of his marriage and that it might be restricting his wife even more than him. Susanna was ten-plus years younger, and although theirs was a sweetly intimate relationship, it was also sweetly patronizing. Her inability to seek a better understanding of herself caused a similar issue with her understanding him. In the aftermath of loosening things up between them, she quickly became attracted, then enamored, by another man only slightly older than her. This process began and ended a number of times for her. The truth is, it was a good thing. At first, Jack found himself alone. It was all a bit confusing. Then Truman came along and he had a conversation he didn't expect to have. A conversation with *Spirit*, except, of course; it was a conversation with himself, but in a very different way. He woke up, and life itself – for him – changed. The insistent question, "Who am I?" wouldn't leave him. After this visit, when he was quiet he heard actual voices talking to him, instructing him, about this question.

Truman instructed that they wait three days after his arrival. On the third day, they didn't eat, and drank only a cedar tea with something bitter in it. Truman told Jack it was a root he'd received from his teacher in South America. It was late May and it was warm in the sun, but still a little cool in the shade. They walked along the long curved beach, out past Fox Island until they came to the mouth of the Kennebec River and followed it inland a bit. In a short while, they found a granite ledge by the river where a scrubby hill behind them rose up about twenty feet. The rock ledge provided a seat in the sun with a little shade, and gave them a view overlooking the river of the pine trees and rocky shores on the other side, and a long view towards the ocean. Jack and Truman took off their coats and laid them down on the warm rock; then sat down on them with their backs against the ledge. Their legs were lit by the sun; their heads and bodies were in a partial shade.

Soon after sitting, they took another drink of tea from Truman's thermos. A few minutes later, Jack felt a warm feeling swell in his stomach and move up his spine to the top of his head, and then seem to flow right out like a water fountain. He looked up and saw the clouds and sun begin to form patterns of slow and flowing tapestries of light, and the air moved like a painting set in slow motion. A gray fox suddenly showed itself by the water across the river, and just as suddenly, a peregrine falcon hovered overhead. It circled three times and came to land on a tall pine tree to their right. It stayed there looking about, and then looked directly at Jack. The fox drank at the river's edge and then moved back and sat, as if to observe. Jack looked over at Truman on his right. Truman was a wiry but strong middle-aged fellow with dark scraggly hair and waiting blue eyes, about five foot ten inches, slight Tolkienesce build, skin with a slight Mediterranean earthy hue, tall with a slight shoulder hunch, a bit of black facial hair and full mustache reminiscent of Mark Spitz. He told Jack that people around here called him The Camel.

Jack had known Truman since college back in the '70s when they studied music at the Hartt School of Music in Hartford, Connecticut. They met the first week of school at night in the cafeteria ice cream line. Jack remembers that Truman ordered pistachio ice cream, something Jack thought was an adult flavor. They got talking and twenty-five years later, they were still talking basically about the same thing – the meaning of life. They invented a formula for success: peace of mind equals simplicity over freedom of mind. It made sense, but often over the years they admitted it escaped them. Truman was obstinate then; he studied English, classical guitar, and then something else, which I've forgotten. He didn't settle down much, but he loved adventure. He moved to New Hampshire, then Maine with a girlfriend he'd gotten pregnant; and settled down working with an insurance company to help people get off workman's compensation and back to work. Truman didn't feel so good about that job, both in the way the insurance company was trying to save money and the way the recipients often had just given up – they were never happy to see you. He still played guitar, singing folk music at various get-togethers. Jack always acknowledged that it was Truman who first taught him about folk music and how to Travis-pick the guitar. In fact, he played his first folk gigs with Truman back then.

Truman sat still cross-legged, his black beard scruffy and hair tossed, his hands on his thighs with his eyes closed as if in a trance; but a smile seemed to cross his lips. Jack couldn't tell how long he'd stayed looking at Truman and the patterns of sun and shadow on his face, but after a while Truman began to talk in a voice that was clearer than anything Jack had heard before. It didn't sound like Truman's usual voice. The voice had a slightly baritone mid-eastern almost Indian accent rather than the slight Maine drawl. It spoke of the power of conversation, a universal language, and healing through energy tones of the human voice.

He paused for what seemed like a long time; then the voice continued. The falcon blinked now and then and kept looking at Jack. Time slowed down and seemed to stop. The *voice* told him what he would do with his life. It told him that he would align with evolution and facilitate the development of a powerful emerging energy point, a Kosmic energy conduit, an undeveloped chakra, located above the heart and over the thymus. This energy point would allow the transfer of a special energy to man. This would permit mankind to better perceive the cause and nature of time. It told him to look for a new school that taught about a community of people with this energy point. "Tap that spot now and then say to yourself, 'I am here'. It will focus you; it helps open the chakra and your connection to all that is."

Truman was silent for a moment and then began speaking, but this time the voice had changed. It was more like an American female voice from the Southwest, in a soft alto. This voice told Jack he would be one of the inventors of a new language associated with this new energy point, and that he would develop a healing energy through voice and dialogue. A language of telekinesis, community, and a new awareness that allows time to be realized in the same way space is.

Jack asked, "Why do we need a new language? What's the matter with the one we've got? "

The falcon walked on the branch and tilted its head towards Jack, staring right at him. Truman remained sitting calmly, his eyes closed. The male voice returned and spoke with authority as if to make a final point, "What you call *life* is an effort to be more and more conscious. Mankind needs a new language because who you are is the language you invent. In order to evolve, you must evolve your consciousness. For this to occur, there must be something different about the language you currently traffic in. This difference takes effort. This is to say, awareness and vigilance. Wake up. Pay attention."

"Where does new language come from?" Jack asked, his stomach becoming a bit tight. He noticed the falcon was still there and at that moment, it seemed to tilt its head and smile. The alto voice returned and said gently, "It comes from you." The falcon looked a little annoyed and the voice added, "New language isn't only about inventing new words. Language lives within the context of conversations and the structure of consciousness. It is what you are conscious of now and what you are capable of that builds this context. Language is the life of consciousness for human beings. Like a plant, it grows; and in different soils or contexts of awareness, it grows differently. When a person speaks to you, you can immediately ascertain what soil their awareness is growing in. If they want to grow differently, they must replant their awareness in new soil. We will help you."

The falcon stood up straight, ruffled its wings, and with one powerful leap, took off. At first circling overhead, then heading east towards the ocean away from the setting sun, towards a peninsula at the edge of the river. Then suddenly, it disappeared from sight. A moment later, Truman opened his eyes and his Maine accent was back. He asked me, "Did you hear the voices, Jack? I've rarely felt anything so peaceful, ... so affectionate." The word peaceful sounded like "puceful;" affectionate sounded like "effect-an-at" with an accent on the "ff."

Jack replied, "This has happened to you before? It was odd; you were talking to me, but not in your regular voice. I didn't know you could speak like that."

"Yes, but rarely. People say I channel something or someone. When it happens, I don't actually hear the voices. I only feel them. So, tell me. What did they say?"

Truman and Jack got up, brushed off their pants, and headed back to the car. Jack went behind a dune and relieved himself. Coming back, he turned to Truman, "I gotta tell you. That was something else. It was as if they gave me instructions – about how to live and what to say." As they walked back home, Jack told Truman what he had heard.

Later that week, as Jack returned and was walking on the beach, he thought he saw the falcon off in the distance, but wasn't sure. At the same moment, he thought he heard the Indian voice in his head, again instructing him about taking care of mankind in the evolution of consciousness. "The evolution of consciousness," he said aloud, as he savored the waves breaking on the beach, the cool sand under his feet, the sun behind him, sand pipers racing, and the upward curve of the beach to the dunes and the hills beyond. It was peaceful and good.

Shortly after, Jack returned to New York City, quit his job, and he and his wife Susanna got divorced. It was the friendliest of divorces. This made it easier on each other on one hand, but like any living thing, ending the marriage had its saddness and loss. They kept living together and helped each other until it was time for Suzanna to move out. He thought, "Thirty years of working and this is where I end up. There's gotta be more." He noticed other things had changed. He had little money, but felt free. He could sense and hear new things. Poems seemed to pop into his thoughts at will. He had a strange experience of sensing what was unhealthy or unsettled about others just by listening to them speak about their lives, and often would hear one of the voices tell him what a person needed for healing. He also discovered that by speaking to people in a different, more intimate way, they would have a conscious shift about their lives. Still, Jack was unsure; he said little about these experiences to others. Truman called him only once, about a month later, and advised him to be patient.

TRUMAN

Truman sat at his desk thinking. "I finished all my work yesterday. So, today I am somewhat *free*. My idea is to clean up my office, dust, and rearrange the piles of academic detritus that haunt the surfaces of my baneful noesis; thereby scrubbing the nether regions of my mind that look a lot like the corners behind my desk where all the electric wires do a spaghetti dance and work in ways I will never fully comprehend, in conditions I cannot acknowledge, in forms of solitude that irk me. I know, by the laws of Feng Shui, that my office depicts my essential being. It conflicts, contrasts and harbors contagions. The calluses of connubial contraband. The pimplin' of cerebral acme. Theoretically, if I clean it up, I clean up myself, unstick the stuck, grease the medulla of my motivations, invigorate the mortitude of nugatory nuggies, nimble and Nubian nubbed and ninevated, like young ass lifted and offered with ease and grace and gratitude." He read a poem from Jack.

Nudiustertian Murmurs

pedal pushers
the drug pins
of everyday
suburban
entropy
that
sounds worse
than they are
As it is
chosen
as we are
Don't forget
how addicted
we all have been
to being
mediocre
tamed and
p-whipped
by what
scares us most
Our
feminine
ennui
ennui
ennui
and,
our fragile
gonatoid gonaditude
your penoid
penchant

for petulance
and the inevitable
limited
limited
limited
performance
in the face
of all
that gimmie
gimmie
shimmie
shimmie
boo bop a lou bop
a-boo bam boo
p-tang
Bless you Osiris
it's enough to
force a man to stand tall
and
froth a
Yes, *Yes*, **Yes!**
and
again
Yes!!

JACK

At this point, Jack was 44 years old. His ex-wife, Susanna, is 34. They divorced a year earlier, and just before his birthday, Suzanna moved to Chelsea. Jack's association with a fellow management consultant, part-time associate, Reissa Maben, was also fading. Both were going off on their own. His divorce was about as amicable as it could be, and they were still good friends. It was harder to connect with Reissa. It seemed they were always negotiating a friendship and rarely coming to an agreement. His week was sporadic. A consulting gig here and there. Enough. Not the daily go-to-work. He liked that. His time was his own. He was more alone, uncertain; but he felt "I'm ok. I'm happy." He was sort of alone. There was Molly who'd attended one of his training sessions a few weeks ago. Sweet, lovely curly girl hair. He'd asked to see her, but she was elusive. They'd had coffee down on East 10th street, she was upset about some other guy, and wouldn't exactly commit to another get together. As Jr. Walker put it, "What does it take to win your love for me?'

Yesterday, on his regular early morning walk by the river, Jack was thinking to himself, and once in a while thought out loud, "Why did Susanna and I split up? Well, I guess it's not unlike the situation with Reissa. We weren't completely aligned and came to the conclusion that we were better friends than partners. With Susanna, we'd accomplished what we set out to in the marriage. We could have gone further in the same old way, but neither one of us would have found what we were looking for. Susanna wanted to find herself and I wanted to start my own business. That was changing me. Looking at it, there wasn't much of an invitation for a mutual future that we both could agree on. That's what Susanna said. Susanna wanted to go one way and I another. We didn't have children so that made it easier. The loneliness was difficult at first, and the whole thing felt illogical. Susanna was strange about it. She seemed to support me, but pushed me away as well. So, we chose to end the marriage, but not the friendship. And now, odd as it is, Reissa and Susanna are lovers. Susanna seems serious but also nonchalant. Not that I mind, and not that the relationship will last, but it does make for some extra drama and goofy explanations to family and friends."

Almost each morning, Jack walked alone. His head was shaved and his beard had grown a bit. When he walked, he always wore his favorite grey cotton sweater. At home in the bale knit; alone in thought, enjoying the morning's fresh chilled breezes. On these morning walks, Jack felt this is the time Manhattan is at its best. Early each morning humming down the sidewalk, people walking in a shekky ground-foot greet. Shekky dance together, away, together, away – Na Na. Hiking to the nimble vistas at the edge of wishful traffic. A poem ran by his thoughts as he watched people go to work. He pulled out a pad to quickly write it down.

traffic lifts dress float hip
round a snarled and empty cheek
against the face of use
early in the morning

brittle lisping wind
licks wimp
amidst the cha cha pulse
and purposeful gallant
of the early riser off to work
painlessly the crease of road
and blackened cornered streets
lay in public prostitution
to the use of many

Later in the afternoon, sitting at his desk, an old refurbished maple kitchen table he had found in the basement; Jack finished writing a report on a training seminar he'd finished last week. He took another walk, bought a falafel, and after a while, found himself sitting on a park bench at the end of the meridian in the middle of Broadway at 104th Street, facing downtown. The sun was bright in stark blue-white-yellow. He sat down, finished the falafel, and thought to himself, "I'm waiting for the next invitation offered by *You* (he looks around), or one that will unfold on the tip of my tongue. An invitation from all this (falafel in his right hand, wax paper around it, he broadly gestures). An invitation that will ripple out upon my oh-so-purposeful tongue. When it arrives I will taste each moment fully and deeply." He sipped rich grainy Turkish coffee from a small paper cup. Steam rose and disappeared around his red baseball cap. The gentle male voice came to him. A familiar voice, not young, not old; male, somewhat Persian. The voice entered his thoughts like an old friend. An intrusion, but as usual, a welcomed one.

"In the taste of awakening, life's mulligatawny sits upon a single tongue. One swift surprising taste occurring again and again. It lingers like an echo. Sometimes lingering in an expanded moment over eternity or its closest relative, a surge of attraction. Sometimes building, ... sometimes fading."

Jack scratched his nose and laughed out loud, and answered the voice, "My attraction right now is for that kicky hairdresser from Denmark I met last week at the Sri Chimoy concert." Realizing he may appear to be talking out loud to himself, he looked around and got up to go home. Upon arriving, he gave Molly a call, only to get her answering machine. He left a message, "Call me."

MOLLY

⟶◆⟵

The day before, Molly had wept intermittently for almost an hour in the corner seat of one of those nugatorium coffee house wimp joints in the East Village not far from her apartment on 10th Street. She wept at the loss of yet another certain mate who declined her interest in him. A married man from Copenhagen who wouldn't leave his wife for her. Just talking about him made her sniffle and cry. She wept in the face of Jack, a stranger she'd just met last week at a concert. She felt lonely and agreed to meet him for coffee.

Her short cropped brown hair with whipped cappuccino curls tugged in a kink of whimsical delight at last night's naughty phone talk. Jack sat across the small round plywood-laminated table stained dark brown and stroked her hand. The one closest to her sense of both hopelessess and desperation. Eager, and feeling attracted to her, he became prophetic and tongue-tied and said anything that would maintain a close proximity.

Molly turned her head and stared out the window across Avenue A at Tompkins Square Park. She rubbed her nose with a napkin. Looking furtively at Jack, she again turned away to clutch the napkin and jealously guarded her sadness, but left her hand in Jack's. "The next relationship will always be better," he said. She believed him and wondered who that might be.

They got up and started walking hand in hand. Jack kissed her on the cheek. They stopped and she kissed his lips. Jack nibbles her ear. She pulled him close. Then suddenly lets go, looks Jack in the face and said, "I can't." Pushes his chest and walks away, head down.

Jack, in a daze, watches her walk away. She turns the corner. Jack startled runs to the corner, but she's gone.

Jack's apartment was quiet. The windows fifteen floors up faced south, letting plenty of sunlight in all day. One beam of light shone behind the piano bench where Jack sat, waited, and sighed, "The dust motes make me sick. And no doubt, I them. Who cares about the blues I play on this old clunker. I'll go for another walk, get a falafel, maybe catch an afternoon matinee." He went over to his desk and looked at a proposal for a community training seminar he just wrote, signed it, and put it in an envelope with $2.23 worth of stamps. Putting on his jacket and an orange cotton scarf he'd bought in Montreal, he grabbed the envelope and walked out.

Molly never called back.

REISSA

Reissa could be a jerk. He tried using flatulent New Age sensitivities to entice Susanna. He succeeded at that, but not for the reasons he believed. Susanna liked coming over from the west side to Reissa's apartment on 6th Street, which was between First and Second Avenues in the East Village.

Susanna told Jack she was on to Reissa's act, but was more interested in the juxtaposition of characters in the drama of her life who might be exposed by sleeping with Reissa. She felt Reissa was almost as much of a ridiculous know-it-all as Jack, but Reissa had a charm and swagger that appealed to her. Jack was a year younger than Reissa with a strong frame and a bald aging Buddha-like look. Something about Jack's eyes were ancient and eastern. He was intuitive and more thoughtful than Reissa, but then, Jack heard voices. Later he called them "guides," and he said they just talked at any time, often instructive and sometimes absurdly poetic. He didn't take them so seriously, but appreciated the comfort and sense of reason they offered. He told Susanna he'd heard voices in the past year.

Reissa was attractive. Nature gave him a full head of golden blond hair, blue eyes, and a tall northern European gaited calm. He might even have known that he didn't have to say a word to impress Susanna. Reissa's chief beauty didn't require a lot of thought. Susanna knew it would seem odd to go out with Reissa, considering he was one of Jack's business partners; but they'd always been friendly and Jack wasn't the jealous type. Reissa was jealous though, she came to discover, and competitive, especially about Jack's success. Reissa was methodical and used specific learned techniques in his consulting practice. He did that well, but was not one to create new things.

Jack was different. He always had new and often provocative ideas in the peculiar way that creative angst cultivates; and the remarkable ability to see nothing in a practical sense and yet go on to invent things and integrate innovative ideas. Jack, at the drop of a hat, created remarkable concepts and analogies out of "the spaces between words." That's what he called it. For instance, Susanna liked to think that he created Reissa as a possible love interest for her, as one day she had shared what most attracted her about men, and the next day she went with Jack to meet Reissa for dinner. It was then the attraction began. That was a month ago. It was pleasing to think Jack did this for her, even if he didn't think so. Jack, on the other hand, hadn't dated much since their divorce; although since Reissa came into the picture, Jack seemed more adventuresome.

⸺◦⟪⟫◦⸺

Around Jack's apartment these past few days, things were often indecisive. He couldn't leave his apartment and he couldn't stay. It felt as if there must be a reason to leave, an invitation. Like an invitation to go get coffee, go to the movies, or give someone a helpful hand. Something like that. Otherwise, he felt stuck, stuck waiting for an invitation. He was hoping for one from Molly.

⸺◦⟪⟫◦⸺

The sun shifted 10 degrees to the right and lit up the edge of the saffron cushion on the piano bench. Jack got up, put on his old gray cotton sweater, looked around as if checking for something important, and then left to go to the roof of his apartment building. The roof was a wide open space above everything else in the neighborhood. The air was cleaner, it was quieter, and you could see far across the Hudson River towards the west. It was one of Jack's favorite places to sit, think, and watch the sun set. It was the main reason he kept the apartment when Susanna left.

THE QUANTUM
THEORY OF LOVE

A few days later, his wool coat pulled tightly against the wisps of fettered midday autumn chill, Jack walked down Broadway and headed for the bench in front of his favorite coffee shop. He enjoyed watching the people walk by. He wore a tight knit gray cotton skullcap that covered his head, his favorite sweater, and the peculiar quizzical frustrations now in total surrender to each step of his life; each moment sustained in a living vortex of separation and immediate want. That's how he felt as he headed for Tom's coffee shop. Back at the apartment, his calls and letters to Molly were not answered. Then, there were Susanna's frantic nonsensical messages on his voice mail about things like the television talk shows she just watched, weather predictions for the day, or most annoyingly, the men in her life. But here on the bench with a cup of coffee, the world anonymously walked by on the wide sidewalk. Occasionally, it sat down to talk with you.

As Jack sat sipping his coffee, a smartly dressed elderly lady hustled over to the bench. She was a proper lady with lightly dyed strawberry blonde hair in a French fold, gray-green tweed suit, and pink and red silk scarf around her neck. In her right hand was a dark, polished wood cane. She paused before sitting down and said politely, "Is there room on that bench for two?"

Jack tilted his head towards her and responded, "Of course, be my guest," and cleared a spot. The lady hovered and dropped her pendulant years with a calculated Manhattan thud.

"82 years," she claimed with Galapagos nonchalance. Eyeing Jack slightly and holding her right knee she said stoically, "A pain I've got in my knee." She further explains, "never had pain ever before; was always young."

"Sorry to hear that," Jack replied, and asked, "Had some bad luck with it this past year?"

"Oh well, not really, but yes in other ways. Friends come and go; you can't stop that. It's up to God." She chuckled into her scarf confidently, but barely audible.

Jack listened, holding back an urge to pontificate on the burdens of omniscience.

The octogenarian settled in and continued, "I have this friend who is 91. She's still around and never complains."

Jack, feeling skeptical, asked, "She never complains?'

"No."

"Oh?"

"Well, yes maybe she complains sometimes. In fact, yesterday, it wasn't much, but you could say she complained."

"About what?"

"She said she was upset because she can't wear high heels anymore! 'I'll have to wear flat shoes like you,' she said to me." And then the lady let out an ostentatious huff, with a distinct sense of incredulity.

"Really?" Jack smiled.

"Now, that's not much to complain about," she said with an odd smirk. "Ah hells bells, it's getting too cold for me out here. I have to go. Nice talking with you." She suddenly got up, said goodbye, and walked off; but not without saying, "The best day of my life."

The wind was slight in the aching early evening and Jack sat for a while and wrote.

A slight wind in the aching early evening
is a simple gesture
of broken lisping invisible weeping
trailed across sidewalks
and into the street
to mingle with a scrap of paper
refuse in the latest twilight
with a groping gaze whip glance toward grace
it shutters
it's the best day of its life

Jack sat on the Manhattan side of the Staten Island Ferry. He liked the ferry; it only required a short ride on the subway downtown and a short walk to the ferry landing. The air was good, the sun comforting; you could relax, and it was free. He realized he was spent, burnt out on diffidence and allegories on the nature of hope. He felt he needed a break, a special gift. He needed an invitation. Instead, in spite of, or maybe in response to everything, he heard the voices in his head modulating between baritone and alto. Now old friends, his best friends. The voices – teaching and confident, poetic and otherworldly. They spoke poetically about philosophy and "other truths", which left him wondering … "Tomorrow never comes."

Weeks had passed since Molly pushed his coffee across the café table. A sign of reluctant gratitude, to push sustenance to an easier grasp. When he told her he loved her, she resisted. Sensing there were no boundaries with Jack, she became annoyed. Jack saw resistance cloud up among her tears that were no longer hers or his, just the weather. But still, he hoped.

He shifted his weight on the bench. He could smell the moldy frit of scam. Had he scammed himself into wanting something he couldn't have? Self-protection dwarfed and tightly clung; his thoughts stalked Molly and today seemed to stalk his every footstep on the pitched and blackened sidewalk in front of him. The female voice began talking to him. *"There's a difference between want and need. Want only gives wanting. Need is essential and revealing. To move forward, you must know the difference."*

"Quantum Theory of Love," the voice spoke on, as if pointing out an interesting tree in the meridian of Broadway. *"The insidious murmur of pent up psychic mud hiding the expansiveness of the Universe, based on the idea that there is only a certain amount of anything and everything available. Pessimism based on a whim, the whim of perception. A limited perception where you see what you get and get what you see and that's all you get. A foolish theory, that there is only as much love and joy in the Universe as any one person can perceive and experience in a lifetime. And, the greed inevitable in this equation – fighting to protect what you have.*

grabbing to get more – the desperate compulsion to get what is lost.

"This theory is the background conversation to every conversation mankind has about itself. A conversation about a dire scarcity of love. We call it the quantum theory of love. But it is a poor theory, a contradiction obscured by muddy thinking. Thinking that obscures the Authentic, the Real, the wholly dynamic expansiveness of everything, of love. This theory thwarts an invitation to affirm, to say 'Yes', and to live an expanded abundant life. It ferments with hope, which feeds distrust. Step beyond and eliminate this theory. It is bankrupt. Trust the Universe and its abundance, rather than hope that abundance exists. It already does. Seek what you need, not what you want.

"Mankind's desire to trust and say 'Yes' is unfortunately obscured by this theory. If you take a look and notice, you will see that the Universe only affirms. 'No' is an illusion, and yet it is a reaction that most describes how humanity lives. If no wasn't an illusion; if it were real, it could <u>not</u> go away. It would remain. It could not be changed, transformed, altered, or removed. 'No' would be like 'yes', unalterable; and all attempts for healing, affirmation, growth, and change would be at odds with the supposed fact that no would be absolute and could not be altered. But, 'No' is not real. Instead 'no' always defines what is not real. No doesn't actually exist, as there is nothing negative in the Universe, including nothing. Negativity is simply the unfulfillment of affirmation, which unfolds with yes There is nothing

wrong with no. At times, it is appropriate. The world opens with 'yes'. Pause, then ask yourself, is 'no' or 'yes' appropriate?

"If mankind wishes to understand the Kosmic Universe, the first step is to take care to notice that the Universe is abundant, the Universe is a yes. 'Yes' is movement. It is an invitation, a quantum affirmation rather than a quantum negation always expanding in embrace and discovering in penetration. All stops, borders, and boundaries that say no exist only as illusions. These illusions are the result of what you do not know and [hence]make up. They are the hesitations of yes. There are no borders, no boundaries, but that which you aspire to. Know what you need and see what you are attracted to. Say 'Yes, that's for me.' If you can't say that, if it is not appropriate, it's not a need and the Universe has little if any interest."

CRABAPPLES ON THE WINDOWSILL

The weekend came around with a late surge of warm weather. Indian summer without green. A wet and lazy harvest slowed the day that wanted no more than a little hurry to a beckoning hidden door.

Jack walked slowly, a walking meditation. He glanced out his kitchen window to the apartment across the street. "Crabapples on my neighbor's windowsill. We had a crabapple tree in the front yard when I was young." He returned to the square red cushion on the floor in the living room. Meditating, breathing, thinking ... "If sitting, just sitting for hours had me finally notice the crabapples on my neighbor's window sill, laid out in a row, largest to smallest, ridiculous and red with embarrassed sweet beet lover's blush and green with gobbled worm-worn hesitation; then I might also dream about my lips touching Molly's fruitful chest and licking her nipples for each separate count of dew. Then tumbling into a first clinging, eye-to-eye connected look and anticipated body-to-body press, pressed and breathed and huddled in a submissive connection." He said to himself, "thinking; return to breathing". He felt odd about the erotic thoughts while sitting. "It happens."

"Connect", muttered through Jack's thoughts with a whip of regret. He sensed a hesitation to listen. *"Release, surrender, pull closer,"* the male voice spoke softly to him, *"grasp the Universe in a grain of sand and hold eternity in a moment."*

"Truman?" Jack asked. "Is that you?" He closed his eyes.

He let his thoughts follow each other randomly. Now and again he saw the crabapples becoming clearer and clearer in his thoughts. Crabapples left as an offering to anything. An offering as simple as the hand that put them there. Why had my neighbor thought to do such a thing? Jack sat in meditation as ancient as the first sitting man and felt his breath stream out from each nostril. Drawn out into such a wasted emptiness to lay the crabapples across his memories. To put them fifteen floors up on an outside window ledge. Not discarded, but laid out against the blue sky. Put there for a chance eye to glimpse. He blinked and the glimpse was gone. The picture of the crabapples vanished. He felt awake and remembered to concentrate on his out breath.

Molly was agitated. She had to go to work at the hair salon on First Avenue and 9th Street and she's late. "Everyone wants everything", she yelled, slamming her palm down on the table next to the computer, and tearing the letter she just wrote from the printer carriage. She began to read out loud her response to Jack ... spun with dirt and deed.

"Jack, I feel sorry about what went on. I literally felt overwhelmed by you. Every time I opened up even a little you took too much. You crossed a boundary. It was just too much for me. Every time I opened up towards you, I felt you came and tried to break down the distance I needed. And, that just doesn't feel good."

Here she thought to add, "you bastard."

"I don't usually tell someone I'll call and then not do it. But as I said, it is just too much. I feel like I would like to leave it as it is and to not have contact with you. Sorry."

She sent the email. Molly banged her ankle on the table getting up and tugged on her hair. She grabbed her leather jacket that she'd bought on the streets of SOHO with Arturo last month when he came to visit her in New York. Arturo, who no longer existed in her life. Arturo and his wife. "Arturo, that bastard!" She slammed the door quickly with sick determination. It whimpered and spit and seemed to chew its splintered nails. It waited, as if it too wanted her back.

———————

Sitting silently in Jack's thoughts, there appeared another picture. A set of beautiful paintings of a dogwood branch in white and pink bloom with a sunlit yellow background. Each set part of five semicircular panels arranged like an arch, hanging on a light creamy sage green wall. Each separate panel showed the dogwood with a continuous but slightly shifted view. The pink, white, and greenish blossoms shifted in each panel. The distance slightly altered from the viewer, who might have been a child or a mouse or another blossoming branch. Or, Jack wanted to believe, a daisy, or a beetle on a daisy. Jack thought about this and saw the pictures as if they were right in front of him, and then let it go from his thoughts. He reminded himself, "I am sitting, breathing, thinking."

———————

Later that day, Jack heard a ballad humming in his head. "Is that Sarah Vaughn singing to me?" Singing soft and slow. Then he heard a song he'd never heard before that sounded like the shamanic alto voice of one of the female guides.

In a wink and tart taste lip
and kiss
humbled and waiting
on a wakeful hello

In the break of our departing
did I ever say there were my sensibilities
fought in folds that shallow your every look?

Did I hear you say
you found me
with an echo?

Then left with comet breath and ease
leaving your crumbs for me to follow

I feel sorry for what went on
I feel sorry for what went on

THE WEB OF CONVERSATIONS

Bok Choy, turnips
ginger, onions, basil,
turmeric
sautéed in olive oil
with a little chicken
over warm basmati rice

Jack mumbled the poem over and over, lit the burners and began to prepare dinner. A thought popped up to call Molly. He resisted, then acknowledged the feelings it stirred before letting it go. He remembered snippets of conversations that fermented during the day. They bipped about in an internal murmer just like the poem, simmering in the elaborate stewpot of the day.

A now familiar male voice took center stage, as if it just walked into the room.

"In the context of the web of conversations that make up the world, the reality we know is a listening phenomenon and dependent upon our listening skills.

The skill of listening to what is said, who says what is said, and what is silently waiting to be said, is the source of mankind's reality. Yet, your relationship to what is real is often wasted due to a lack of skill in honoring your perceptions and potential. There is no authentic reality in speaking. It is in your listening that reality is fulfilled. And, although what is heard is spoken unauthentically and then only as a reflection, it is your access to power and presence in this world."

"Why do these thoughts come now?" Jack questioned himself while gently shaking the savory mixture in the heated pan.

The sudden yet persistent voice entered Jack's thoughts again. It spoke in slow and deep murmurs, as other voices had done since as far back as he could remember, always guiding him. Guides, ancient foreign voices that mingle with his thoughts and words. Often inventing word sounds and language in interwoven prattle. Guiding him as if the ocean or a remote quasar were speaking to a favorite son. But, this voice was different and always brought him back to that river in Maine with Truman, sitting in the half sunlight with his eyes closed. He listened.

"Authenticity occurs in immediate listening. To listen for the presence of what is here and now is a great skill. Everyday chatter must be quieted. A silence occurs and a glimpse of Authentic Reality is revealed. An immediate present-ing of existence as it occurs is revealed in this

form of awareness. When listening is immediate, and in each moment complete and totally fulfilled with what is so in each moment, you are present to all of human experience and possibility. You are at the end of perception known and spoken, and on the edge of what can be known and is unspoken. You are at the edge of what we call 'droxis.' Here, the language of the Universe is invented. This may occur only as a glimpse or a word, yet it is enough to cause new worlds to exist. For some, whole discourses are available and Universes are born. It is worth striving for.

"The practice that gives access to understanding this skill is twofold: 1) notice the role you choose and the conversations that follow, and 2) be available to the promise of life. That is, declare a commitment to live life fully and to be attentive to what is happening. A true promise is essentially a complete willingness to be available for the discovery of authentic and complete reality, to go beyond hope and unveil trust. This discovery is not personal and it cannot be found alone. Therefore, neither can a promise be made alone. It is your speaking with others that creates your listening. In true dialogue, you are able to acknowledge the in-between space, between listeners, where conversation powerfully dwells. Eternity exists in these spaces and the full dimensions of time are revealed. The power to exist in the in-between, in each moment, and in every moment, is accessed by the energy field around the heart. Listen with your heart and wisdom will be revealed.

"Most people are not aware they have the ability to promise, let alone see the capability of a promise to create power. There is little education or accountability for it in the world of human culture today. Though education about this is rare, there are some who teach it. They teach mankind this: In speaking about your lives, your life story, it doesn't need to be so neatly tied up. It only needs to be genuine in each moment. You say what is happening or going to happen, and by when it will happen."

A line of a poem he'd written two weeks ago flits by Jack's thoughts.

battered hope
and wilted want
forgot the slight and silky breeze
today is a promise
lost in knowing hands

Pouring the contents bok choy, red bell pepper, sweet onion, baby spinach and cashews from the pan onto a white ceramic plate with blue lettering that reads, "Blues is Best," Jack remembered that Gabriella, a woman he'd met at one of his training seminars two weeks ago, was coming over tomorrow to pick up information on the seminar. He remembered her as being about 35 years old, slender but full-figured, with soulful deep brown eyes and pleasant wavy shoulder-length dark brown hair, and a joyful air about her. He thought to himself, "pretty girl that one, good armful she is."

He looked around the one-bedroom apartment. The plate of food lay steaming on top of a round blue tablecloth that covered the café table in a small nook. His living room, which is adjacent to his bedroom and his office, lies a lush Persian rug in dark blues and borders, holding in an array of golden flowers and green vine designs. On one side of the room, a Victorian sofa with flower prints in pink on a gold background rested aside a comfortable red velvet armchair. A spinet piano in soft browns whispered on the opposite side of the room from the sofa, and his desk in the middle against the wall with computer, fax, scanner, and printer on it. His black metal filing cabinets stood against the wall, and the large black leather executive's chair seemed to wait for a king or a duke, or an earl. A large ornate mirror covered almost the entire wall above the sofa and the windows are draped in deep blue satin with delicate white curtains behind them. An antique round table, a jade green Vietnamese ceramic end table that was shaped like a royal elephant with an elegant platform on its back, Japanese ink pictures of birds, and an antique breakfront filled the room. It was a cozy place to talk and work.

Before eating, Jack sat for a minute in silence.

THE INVITATION

Gabriella is Portuguese. She arrived with a Greek girlfriend for lunch, and Jack prepared a neat dish of nuts, Stilton cheese, and seedless grapes.

"Gabriella, it's good to see you," Jack greeted them, taking their coats and hanging them in the foyer closet. Both were in their mid-30's.

Turning to the Greek, Jack asks, "It's nice you came along. I'm Jack. What's your name?"

Nestling into Jack's red velvet overstuffed chair, she answered politely, "Tess, from Philadelphia. I'm up for the weekend helping Gabriella with her clients. I do energy work and therapeutic massage too." She dropped a grape into her mouth and chewed.

"Oh, it's great to meet you, Tess. I'm originally from Philadelphia. I didn't know Gabriella did bodywork." Jack smiled at her and handed Gabriella a neatly bound report. "You do bodywork?"

Gabriella took the report and put it in her knapsack. "Well I did, but now I do a form of energy healing that combines prana, chi gong, polarity, cranial sacral, and my own version of divine healing. With my technique, I balance a person's energy at various levels from deep within, and out past their auric field. I only lightly touch the person's body. Tess and I studied together a few years back. To do energy work well you have to practice, learn to listen to the Universe, and ask the right questions. Recently, my clients started picking up, and it looks like I can do this more full-time. Tess is helping me this weekend to get my files and office straightened up."

"That's odd; I mean wonderful." He hesitates and turns to Tess, "Did Gabriella tell you how we met? He asked politely, but continued before she answered. "She was at one of my training retreats for the Board of Directors of the local business improvement district. My associate, Reissa, introduced us." Looking suspiciously at Gabriella he said, "As I recall, he had a thing for you."

With delicate plump attention, Tess sat carefully on the couch. Her hair combed neatly back in a brisk of blended perfect mocha, coffee-like with two splashes of cream. The curve of her body draped in a long dress, fruity like a pear. She smiled impishly and added, "Yes, she told me. Your business partner, Reissa ..." She answered with a knowing hint of pepperell, "called Gabriella erotic." She drew out the rrrrr laughingly, washed and eddied in a vale of peach, apple, and ripe pears.

Gabriella, having moved to the carpet, was twisting in yogic stretches. "Loosening up." A nervous rip in her washed brownlit, light, and lighted eyes; chin perked and suspiciously pestered by lapping late night dark molasses hair drenched with last night's sleepy rich lateness; tight cotton pants pulling and holding her hips like an urn; she responded to Tess's comment, "Well the truth is, he emailed me after the training. He said he was attracted to me. At the seminar, he had told me he was attracted to me. I was flattered but told him I wasn't interested. He seemed upset and followed me around. When I talked to you, Jack, he made sounds like he was jealous. I don't know why he emailed me afterwards. Besides, ..." with a quick wishful glance at Tess, then looking at Jack, she added shyly, "I find you more appealing."

"Oh, thank you." He looked at her, but only caught the corner of her eye as she turned to Tess.

Gabriella and Tess went on to tell stories in a dimpled know of lust and betrayal. Jack poured tea prepared in seed and dust. The quiet confines of incense tweaked their noses. Pheromones, young with grape bled moistful brood waited in the folds of the most gentle; but mocked the sternum gallantly.

Gabriella got off the floor and came to sit near Jack on the Victorian sofa. Its corners of carved intricate dark wood and golden cloth with pink roses curved deep to allow a closer turn. Here, hope found a nest, and Jack put his hand over Gabriella's hand. They seemed to move magnetically, their hips touched astride a crunch of fugitive potato chips. Tess smiled and dipped her head as she looked at Gabriella. Jack felt he saw a wink pass between them. He leaned slightly and whispered into Gabriella's ear, "I'm attracted to you." Gabriella's head dipped and she looked back quickly at Tess.

A poem ran through Jack's mind …

> *little sit and sit so close, and*
> *still you want*
> *but, if you want what you get*
> *you want no more*
> *and … in each moment*
> *the silk brush gives and gives*
> *a small leg touches your leg*
> *there you'll find the light rain gentle*
> *with a simple smile*
> *on a fairie wisp*
> *you shine*

Jack, feeling a breeze, stood up to close the window. His thoughts, jazzing and bopping, raced through the delicate offense of occasion.

> *yip flies when*
> *jeff tenders a longing look*
> *he settles in attraction's yips*
> *speaks them tenderly*
> *and each by name*

Across town in the East Village, Susanna surrendered. That's what she called it, and that is what it was. Reissa, in deep belief of ownership, collapsed in a pool of humor and was loved. He greeted her femoral artery with his swelling tongue and bound himself in chains of tender highs balanced on a sweeping river. Back cleaved hasty by want, "I want." The noise beat him senseless and dumbed him to her need.

"What did you say?" Susanna pouted gingerly.

"Did I say something?" Reissa perked up.

"Yes, I think you said, 'I miss my version of your sweet touch.' How odd, to miss what hasn't gone."

"That's exquisite," whippled Reissa, feeling cool, as the slight cotton tee shirt slipped between his fingers in a tickling babe-tug shiffle.

After leaving Jack's apartment and on the way to the subway, Gabriella turned to Tess and said, "I like Jack. I like him a lot."

Tess looked at Gabriella, "I know you do. There's something about him. He seemed to like you a lot." The wind whipped cold and Gabriella put her arm through Tess's as they hurried to the subway.

Tess asked, "What did he whisper to you?"

"He said he was attracted to me."

Tess laughed, "Yeah, like I said, I think that was obvious."

⋘⋙

GINGKO TREES

It was after midnight as Reissa swept the floor of his tiny apartment – a six-floor walk-up on East Sixth Street closer to Second Avenue than First Avenue, bathroom out in the hall. In the apartment a sink widened as a bathtub, two rooms, and a large closet. He would sleep in the loft in the kitchen area. It's quiet there away from his living room, which was also his office. The apartment faced south; the window was open to let in a bit of the evening air. He has lived here over eleven years, on and off. Even when he went to Mexico for two years, he kept the place. A half-eaten quiche Lorraine sat on the table, grinning at a half-eaten pear.

Reissa pondered Jack's email about the "Quantum Theory of Love," and felt annoyed. "Jack, who connects so well with people in his training groups also says and writes the strangest things. He says he hears voices, songs, poetry. He's not afraid to tell people about this. But it's so strange. Who does he think he is, Socrates or the prophet Isaiah?"

Earlier that day when Susanna had been over, Reissa asked her what she thought about Jack. Answering Reissa's question, "Jack is different," she said. "Yes, in some ways he's not normal. That is, not the same as other people. Not crazy, just different. He behaves differently. Not because of what he thinks or says he hears, but because he isn't afraid to share it. I think sometimes I am the only person who gets him. I don't always understand the actual words, but there is a definite meaning I get out of them. It takes courage to use language that way, and probably more courage to share it with others. Reissa, there's something about Jack that's unique and someday may be important."

"I don't know; Jack's pontificating annoys me," Reissa responded, stiffening up. "In a way, yes, I see what you're saying. But my perception is that Jack isn't understood that well by others. And if you say it's a different style, you deny the fact that he isn't really connecting with others. I mean, I'm glad he and I are still friends, but why is what he says so important to you Susanna?"

She looked back at Reissa and chewed her lower lip, smiling, "Ok, I'll try again. I'm left with a definite feeling that it's not the traditional way of saying things and yet, by the time I've heard it, I know what he means. And yes, he isn't always clear and that has gotten to me at times too. But over the years, he is getting clearer and I think it may simply be a matter of him accepting himself." Susanna reached for a pear, took a bite, but left most of it uneaten."

Pulling on his socks, Reissa rocked on the futon in the living room and looked at his desk. The desk was a panel of flat wood about six feet long and three feet wide on two filing cabinets jammed into the far wall and up against the corner by the window. He let his thoughts drift. Just yesterday, he'd noticed the Gingko trees were dropping their yellow leaves. Gingko leaves, prehistoric fans owned by large wasps, the sort of fans large wasps might carry. He looked at his desk again. An old computer and half-used papers were all over the desk – a dubious collage of frantic love letters, most of them written to Susanna. He turned and looked fiercely towards Susanna.

"Jesus, Susanna!! I don't think you're honest with him." Reissa glared at her, his hair falling across his face. He brushed it back quickly, "If you would give him more feedback, like I do, Jack and you could experience much more. Why do you keep yourself from that? I like him a lot. What I don't like is his neurotic preaching. He has delusions of grandeur sometimes. I prefer not to be in touch with that so much because it feels like, ..." he hesitates, "well, like scattered energy to me." Reissa looked out the window, "You idolize him. Wake up. This is your trip, to idolize people. Come on, wake up. He isn't that great."

Susanna was notably agitated, "My, my, what's eating you? Jack may be strange at times, but he's not neurotic. You of all people know that. I don't idolize him, even if I do admire him. I didn't divorce him because he's neurotic. If anything, it was because of me. Nobody is goofy here; that's not the issue, so don't go there." She got up and paced a bit before sitting down next to Reissa. She looked his way. He stared ahead.

Slowly she edged closer, sat down, and suddenly threw her leg across his, leaned over, put an arm around him, and kissed him on the neck below his ear. She whispered into his ear, "Reissa, it's not really true what you're saying about Jack. Besides, you know I admire you too." She stroked his hair away from his face, admiring his slight Nordic eye fold. "Actually, he connects very well with people. Of course, not everyone. You and I don't always connect well with everyone either, but the truth is that plenty of people really do connect well with him." She pauses, "and, with you too." She continued, "I constantly give Jack feedback and I don't always agree with him. I'm not afraid to say when I don't agree or when I do with anyone." Reissa remained still and again Susanna paused, then snuggled into his neck, and ran her lips from chin to folded eye. Her voice softened, "I know it's not how you'd like it to be, and I can imagine it's not fun. But, believe me, you're not competing with Jack or he with you."

Reissa relaxed. He turned towards her and nuzzled her face. She said to him, "I like the way we flow. We have a nice energy and I'm happy to be with you. To be honest, I feel very close to you, and I feel I have to live my life. Let's just leave it alone. OK? Right now, I'm tired and have to get back home and work on an application for a fellowship to study in Paris. When I get there, I hope to read a nice email from you."

His hand fell flat against the guide of her hip. The lead of humus turned, as silky knowing mud.

—◅◖◗▻—

Purpled dank evening shrugged in deep blue, swinging low in the wash of setting sun as Susanna left Reissa's apartment building. She went down the short steps to the sidewalk and headed towards the 14th Street subway. The urgent smell of satisfaction teased her with warm buttery chocolate as she passed the bakery. Turning onto First Avenue, a blanket of cooking curry molested her happily as she walked by an Indian restaurant. She continued on past a dark and waiting dive bar, an herbalist weighing serious looking stickets and twigs, and a new age hair salon before stopping to buy her favorite regina biscuits and almond biscotti. Susanna then hurried on, as the crying sand-scratched brush of leather shoes trotted across the sidewalk – the walkway splattered with black pressed chewing gum, pigeon shit of gummy choking pleas, wobbled squishy clichés, and other avoidances of sincerity. Markers of conversations that failed to appease.

Susanna glanced at the lights in the window of Lanza's Italian restaurant. The tables were set for dinner – white tablecloths with smaller red ones crossed on top; pink carnations in bud vases next to bottles of olive oil, red wine vinegar, and slender glass shakers of salt and pepper; no silverware. The perfume of roasted garlic, stewing olive oil, and pepper settled enticingly around her. Her stomach warmed and she tasted the swollen call of pasta. As she walked, her mouth was full of delight. "Mmmmmmm ..." she hummed a cascading mantra, burying deeper and deeper into the composting "squirm" of earth and sex, belly to belly, body-to-body, whisper to fading whisper. She remembers nibbling on Reissa's ear, "chewy," and she headed down into the subway station for a train across town.

Back in his apartment, Reissa took a piece of paper off his desk. It's the beginning of a letter. Subject: Goodnight. From: Reissa, To: Susanna. He bent it slightly in the middle and, leaning over to the floor, swept up a small pile of dust.

PEARS

——◄━═╣▌▐╠═━►——

At 6 o'clock, Jack awoke. His bedroom window
faced the Hudson River on West End Avenue
and he had a clear view to the river, New Jersey,
and beyond. The sunrise was a filigree of western
colors, backlit by the dawn, streaming crinoline
veils of tenderness, moving and delicate degrees
of affection reflected off the Hudson and bracketed
by the river banks. As sweet as morning warmth.
He rose.

He dressed in old black, paint-spattered khakis
and the old dark gray sweater he wears all the time
now that it is getting colder. Barefoot, he put on a
battered pair of leather Timberland moccasins, a
down-filled midnight navy coat, and a blue knit
hat. He walked two flights up to the roof and
watched the sunrise.

Half to himself and half to the morning, he said,
"If all my feelings and thoughts were like this
rising sun, if each moment rose in the sweep of this
awakening, and flowed with the gentle warming
hues of this sunrise, this invitation; I would face

each moment with great joy and anticipation of this same tender gentleness, this simple goodness."

He thought of Molly and her silence towards him, and smiled until his heart broke. He smiled, feeling the sun warm and yellow press against the lightness of his eyes. In his thoughts, he saw the quick twist of Molly's first hello and her reluctance for more than a kiss. His emptiness she called a need. In a sense, it was a dream born less from something new than a pregnant surrender to find missing light and warmth. He felt a pressing frustration rise with each memory. But it was uncertain recollections, not like the reality of this sunrise. He felt foolish, and felt foolish about feeling foolish. "How old do you have to be to accept this?"

Jack felt lost. His imagination stumbles through the gates of frustrated murk and landed like a jerk on Molly's tilted concerns. She couldn't move quickly enough and spit a sour taste from her gut. The tortured longing for a touch long gone. He was a surrendered man bound to jagged rocks. Cragged. He felt empty and drank sober venom with a desert wish. "It's best to be alone," he nods to the supple horizon.

Into the well of sunrise, he clasped his hands in prayer, facing north, left thumb over right thumb. He stood straight and loose, and slowly lifted his arms as he began Tai Chi. He felt morning's created breath as it streamed from his fingertips in an arching graceful dance. As the early sunlight's reflection bathed against the western sky, he moved slowly on the roof and within the Universe, as if underwater. The colored air's shameless first light began to billow with purposeful design from the east. A pair of doves arched across the sky at its zenith in a tidy swim. Jack, in gentle balance, reached for a distant apex somewhere in the depths of outer space. Then he let go to push a speck of dust from opened fingertips. He greeted the South and North, the East, the West; and settled back into a gentle dissipating breath, blown as if by moss not man. There he stood, to be a blessed son.

⟞⟝

Molly woke and turned in bed. She pulled her quilt up to her chin and sighed. In her mind's eye, she sees herself accept Jack's kiss when he said goodbye at the café. She dipped, so the kiss landed north and west of her lips, and then, only with a struggle. It stung her to reject him, and woke her with a crack of whip. Anger came to flood the fallen tree, and dulled the wash her shower had intended.

⟞⟝

Jack returned downstairs and heard someone singing 16 floors down on the street. Maybe it was the French woman from Madagascar he met in the lobby yesterday, with her throaty swallowed desperate voice. She said she was a singer. But this song was like a morning tune on a wooden flute. It pushed into his apartment with nonchalance to the corner of the kitchen near the aloe plant. Its daggered tongues as lick and dry with spider-sit in a clay pot of brown and gold, cutting Chi, touching but not reaching. He went to the computer. The singing mingles with the reveille of brewing coffee, toast popping, and Jack's fingers tapping on the computer. The keyboard popping like a woodpecker chorus, expectant and determined drums intent with loaded charm, turned the quartet into a tango. He typed it out.

sparkled bothered bits of nonsense
shuffling dust moat debris
coffee grounds at the bottom
tealeaves on the walls
stirred and waiting materials
tomorrow's earths
from which tomorrow clings
desperately
to seek a hushed and endless lair
hung in a beam of sunlight
dust
nervous intruders
caught in a prison break

Molly checked her email. Another letter from Jack.

He wrote, "What are you talking about, 'no contact?' Are you still in the city?"

———

She ignored Jack's email, sipped her coffee, ate her toast, and settles on thoughts of last night, "How nice it was to hold that guy last night. What was his name? Freddy?"

The sun, which can't be seen from the second story because her window is blocked by buildings and more buildings, managed to find its way into her apartment. It's bright this late morning and lit up the acrylic painted bright green kitchen table with a computer and printer, glue stick, scissors, and a mouse on a burgundy pad. Molly reached over and grasped the mouse. Her hand settled into a familiar caress. With a bent back, she slightly twisted the mouse, paused, and with her index finger hit delete. She adjusted her loose robe and pulled it around herself tightly. Tugging at the collar and lapels, she felt for a second the softness of her breast, slight and firm. Her hand settling into a familiar caress – reflex, index finger press, pause. "Eddy, that's his name."

———

In his East Village apartment, Reissa flipped a buttered egg in a frying pan. His long blonde hair slicked, licked, and clinging like a wig to his slender neck. Just out of the shower, he pulled a towel closer to his waist. His hands clasped the towel right below his belly button; a strong back swooped in graceful arch and furrowed Hudson dare. In the toaster was the nut bread his neighbor gave him when his grandmother passed away. Sad to hear that, but great bread. Coffee was in a French press stewing. Organic sugarless soymilk bought the day before stood alert and at attention on the top fridge shelf. Outside, a workman's premorning quiet settled by the window and murmured in luscious tones of ready but not moving. Two pears ripening on the window ledge; he reached for one of them. His hand settled on it, pear in palm, index finger on the stem.

⚊⚌⚋⚍⚊

Having gone out for a short walk and returned, Jack walked out of the elevator, drifted down the hall, entered his apartment, and closed the door, as if he was patting a good friend on the back. He hung up his coat and hat, and went into the kitchen for a cup of coffee. Finding a mug, he first poured a small amount of soymilk in and then the coffee. He found a pear in the fridge and ate it slowly; then returned to his desk. He picked up the telephone and called Reissa, while staring at the blank computer screen in front of him. It rang twice and Reissa answered.

"So, what do you think about my piece on scarcity and the "Quantum Theory of Love? I'm thinking of using it in a new seminar." Jack asked Reissa.

Reissa paused, then said, "Honestly, I'm only about a third of the way through your emails. I'm beginning to like it, though I had a bit of a hard time at first. You may be on to something here, but a lot of this has been said before. Also, with your prose, I believe you get too carried away with the scat and are hard to understand. Work on making it refreshing, but not distracting. Plus there are too many bullshitty adjectives. Be more succinct, like a bullet."

Jack shook his head and responded, "I hear you Reissa. I'm working at it. Right now I'm just writing it out as it comes to me. Some of this stuff is already around, yes, but it's also a fresh conversation. At least for me. I get the sense it's all going towards something, if not new, something clearer. There's something emerging in my writing and thoughts that are inventive. As if inventing language, new ways of describing things. Reissa, I'm not even sure I'm making this stuff up. It just comes to me. Can you dig it?"

"I don't know Jack. What's the point? I don't understand you sometimes. I'm not sure you've established the credentials to do that. It seems you purposely mis-use language. It's unique, but it's not good writing. It sounds like you degenerate into pop philosophy that's been said before and better." Reissa felt satisfied.

"Like I said, I hear you Reissa, but trust me on this one. Stay open, OK? Anyhow, I called to invite you and Susanna both to the schvitz. You know, the Russian baths down your way."

"Both of us? Yeah sure," Reissa agreed.

Jack hung up, feeling tightness in his chest. "Maybe Reissa's right. Maybe I should give up." He paced a bit and shook his head. "No, he isn't. Not completely. There's something else bugging him. When that passes, he'll come around."

THE SCHVITZ

A drop of blood billowed in a peek from Jack's
fingertip. A rich lady's ruby perched on flesh.
He tested with the glucose meter and monitored
the octane shift of sugar stored to flame and
burn within the confines of his beating heart.
Each explosion a diabetic death, each puff of
snort belt thimbled mince, curled lip, a bombing
lunch. Each scratch, a funeral fogged in by the
next death. He laughed and sent a billion peaks
of humor to their deaths. He sat and pressed pity
into dust. He shivered on the roof and cracked
the glass of panic's beaten pun. This life a ruin of
potential, poppies in a piss about their position
on the stage of life, as pissed as prick blood bloom
and gurgle. "You can go gently into that night,
but why would you?"

Reissa and Susanna agreed to meet Jack at the
Russian baths on the Lower East Side. It's deep
in a basement oven-heated cement-tiered sweat
joint. Water spickets built in with 5-gallon plastic

buckets to catch the water and pour it on your head before you cook into a tasty poached egg stew.

Coming over on the L-Train underground, sitting waiting for the train, Reissa was arguing with Susanna about biting his fingernails. Explaining to her how it is a reaction to doubt, an incessant choice and phaseshift want.

"It's a doubting thing, like, is it this or that? Do I want this or that? You know, when you see you can go in more than one direction at once, say something one way or another. Well, I believe I hold my choice about things a second longer than most. At least this is what I see myself doing and my reaction is a hesitating anxiousness. So, I bite my fingers," he said quickly. "Get over it."

Suddenly, Susanna looked behind Reissa and gasped. Reissa turned around and there was a middle-aged, very dark skinned Haitian man in a business suit right behind them slumped a bit to the side. A pale silence passed unnoticed and passed like a palm across the slumped unhappy shoulders, past the stiff laid neck and lightly matted his short and curled hair.

A woman, apparently his wife, tragic and strangely empty; stood with three Firemen who were attempting to lift the man. They were tired in slow-motion dread. He was dead weight. He's dead. "How did you get him off the train?" one fireman grunted.

"I don't know,, her voice shaded from a deeper place, a place of time spent over breakfast just that morning. The annoyance that snapped as quickly as the toast that broke when the knife full of butter pressed heavy on the blackened bread.

"He took his insulin this morning. On the train, complained of a chest pain and I helped him off the train."

"He died right behind us when we were talking", Susanna whispered. Reissa jumped up, "You're kidding? We were just talking and I didn't hear a thing."

Susanna, hands to her mouth, eyes bright, "Jesus, this is creepy."

Suddenly, on the other track the train arrived and they both hopped on.

The Russian bath was hot, heated by a huge built-in stone oven in the corner, as tall as the cement room. Reissa dumped a bucket of cold water over his head. Bare chested, Jack sat in loose blue shorts, head hung in the heat, a wet towel over his head, a sultan in a secret cave. Susanna joined them. She had on cotton spa shorts and a dark green robe. Reissa walked over and sat down next to Jack.

"Are you OK?" Reissa asked.

Jack answered, "Yeah sure. Love this heat."

"Yeah it's great. I mean are you OK? How are you feeling?"

"Great!" Jack looked at him.

"I mean about Susanna and me," Reissa continued.

Susanna looked at Jack and put her hand on his knee. "Yes, Jack. How are you?"

"Hey, what's the sudden concern? I'm fine. I'm very happy for you two. What's your point?" Jack grabbed a bucket of water and dowsed himself.

"I don't know Jack; you seem distant?" Susanna asked with wilted concern.

"What? Yes, of course." Looking back and forth at both of them, "No, I'm just a little hot here obviously. You two seem to be doing well. I don't think that's a surprise. I'm glad to see you both together." Turning to Reissa, "and Reissa, we may have some consulting work to do with First National Bank. If you're still interested?"

All three grabbed a bucket of water and poured it over their heads.

A few minutes passed. Reissa finally said, "Yes, of course."

They sat for a while in the sweat stroke steamy grunge of spa-heat and burnt evaporated sweat. Back weighted mind drugged in slow bent wet water dungeon, dripping wet floors, tangled oak leaves like placid turds soggy limp congregate around the drains. Heated up noodle among splatted time wasted nothings. "Take me, ... take me!"

Reissa still felt Jack was hiding his feelings. But, Jack left for a deep cleaning soap massage and later remembered only long fingernails tickling his spine. The spa massage, a bathed infant wash. Massage with its degrees of affection. "Ok. Yes." And, there he lay naked and took his wash as privately as the masseuse gave, gentle laps of seated fevered dig and swell. Pulled welted wing and pleasant take.

Susanna dwelled in brine between these men. Jack noticed Reissa's sense of win and sees it isn't moving. When they left, Jack held Reissa in a long embrace. Reissa waited, knowing he would hide and so could not hold Jack as long, and broke first. Something's amiss. Susanna walked away, hand in Reissa's hand. The ease in her step was honest.

TRASH

Walking around the city, Jack couldn't help noticing that sometimes it seemed as if there was trash everywhere. Trash scattered in the hallways, stacks of dump out in the streets – thrown about by some beast disguised by the night and somehow made glorious in the last details of trash. Trash strewn, trash tucked away. Trash picked sifted and thrown like the panhandled mud of latent transient usury. Trash between worlds of trash. When the power shifts, trash goes out the door, trash goes outside, trash is dumped and burnt and freed. Free but not as innocent as the fallen yellow Gingko leaf mélange under foot, blowing around, flattened on the sidewalks, smashed by passersby, schmeared and laying prostate. The leaves welcoming feet pushing through them. They separate and lift gently up from this earth. Shooting a path of settled pure yellow that lifts a brilliant greeting to a man's yarns. The trash, it tells a different story. All about a burning array of trash and leaves. The desert of destiny. A tilted post-traumatic interlude left behind. A puniness that rots away when winter comes.

—⊸◊◊◊◊⦚◊◊◊◊⊸—

Molly licked her fingers. Half a rotisserie chicken mounts her plate and Molly tucked a slice of bread in eager supper. A biscuit with a pat of butter between her bites of chicken melted bird.

—⊸◊◊◊◊⦚◊◊◊◊⊸—

Unanswered mail tasted of fallen Gingko leaves and trash. Burnt mélange. A trash that sits through eternity with sick, waiting grief. Pining magnificent against a sunset of rosy sweat like teased often tortured want. Blessed by brief release and called virtue. Yet the mail remained unanswered, and Jack knew an answer would not come. No matter how bright or bent on admiration the flaming burning trash may be, it is lost when a heart is broken by the absence of a kiss. Never was it heard, "I admire you," or "And I you." In that absence, Jack could see why the trash kept flowing.

—⊸◊◊◊◊⦚◊◊◊◊⊸—

It's dark on the roof. Jack sat there in a lawn chair after sunset. He thought, "Maybe the last yellow Gingko leaf has dropped. Falling back and forth. Tilting in an unknown, never answered breeze. Falling to a hand that smells of dusty churchy incense. Falling on a finger forgotten just like a breeze that licks a rounded cheek where a tear just fell." A Gingko leaf of fanning yellow drip could hide a tear that never answers letters.

Molly pulled a drumstick off the crusted tired bird, biting slowly at the easy meat flaking properly towards her lips. She loved the sweet and juicy wings, crunching on the shallow candy bones. Yet she picked at the rest here and there, and left a lot of meat on the heavier structured frame. She couldn't quite finish. In the trash it went.

SUSANNA

The morning brought a bright gray-fogged autumn as fine rain lathered the rooftops of Manhattan. Vague leaves painted a forest; peeking here and there were blue, black, red, and green colored umbrellas floating along the sidewalks below. Purposeful star movement, affectionate colors in the dripping gray.

Susanna stood at her bedroom window, cup of tea in hand, looking at the street below. Dressed only in green satin bra and gray cotton underwear, she'd just arrived from her shower. Her dark hair with auburn highlights was cupped in wet toweling, regal around her head. Separated by the thin glass, she watched the umbrellas, legs poking out hurrying by on the street below. She's waiting for Jack. Jack is coming by with her part of the sale of their boat, proceeds from the divorce. "Great times waterskiing on Lake Champlain."

Brushing her teeth, Susanna remembered Jack's approach. The spreading warmth behind her like honey dipped by spoon into tea lifting with a steam sweet breath, the ownership of places often traveled. The shower's moist heat held a lingering stir, and the rain settled in ponds on tinseled roofs. As the rain dripped down the window, Susanna drank her warm tea mixed with milk. She put on a kimono-style robe.

⚜

Jack walked to Susanna's apartment. He remembered walking through the street fair last week and finding a tarot card reader in her gypsy shawl, an old lady wrapped with scarves and a long flowing multi-colored skirt. The lady had said to him, "this is a time of vulnerability." As he walked, a familiar voice spoke.

> *this is a time of vulnerability*
> *of an open heart*
> *awakened*
> *to a sudden rush*
> *of movement*
> *in a world gone slightly mad*
> *and I'm a goner*
> *I go through this*
> *time of fearlessness*
> *of touch and move through sadness*
> *touch and then let go*
> *lean into the sorrow as if to almost fall*
> *and lift the chin up*
> *breathe*
> *and follow this gentle wind*
> *breathing in a world gone blind to goodness*

and I am a goner
I go through this

this is a time of wetness
of a moist surrender
beginning
placed in the hues of spectral weep
stirred with honey
warm as tea
lifting with a steam sweet breath
a reflection
in a world gone background gray
umbrellas like tilting stars
and I find
I am a goner

—◅⦿⦿◌◌▻—

Jack buzzed Susanna's apartment, waited for her hello, entered the building, went up the elevator and knocked on her door. He knocked twice. On the third beat, Susanna opened the door, they smiled, held both hands together, shared a quick kiss and a long remembered hug.

—◅⦿⦿◌◌▻—

Susanna moved out a year ago to find a little peace, to break what she called "a pattern of being in a relationship that was closing in on her." It wasn't fun anymore to be so settled, or be just a wife and nothing else. A dummy in a play written by someone else. Known only as what was designed or cooked for dinner, already cooked. At first she resented Jack, but soon realized it was her judgments of herself. All the ought-have-beens and ought-to-bes of wifery, so deeply learned. Later she saw her marriage to Jack as just a prop for that old and worn out design. She left him in September to relax and break the mold. And yet, they never tired of talking to each other.

—⬥—

Entering Susanna's comfortable apartment, Jack looked about approvingly, "Hey Susanna, how're ya doing?"

"Pretty well." She walked over and hugged him again, kissing him on the cheek and staying with this kiss a moment until her teeth behind her lips could feel the angle of his jaw. "Want some tea?"

Jack noticed her fresh cleaned hair, and standing up straight smiling said, "Sure, … your hair smells nice. By the way, you and Reissa seem to be doing well."

Susanna walked to the kitchen, turned around, and slowly crossed her arms, "Yes, he's a good man."

"Yes, he is," Jack responded easily and sat on the sofa.

Susanna paused and looked straight at Jack, "But Jack, really, are you upset about this?"

Jack stopped and shook his head in a meager horizontal determination, then sighs, "Am I supposed to be? In our own ways, you know, we both wanted this."

"Uhmmm," Susanna retreated suspiciously.

Jack added, "Honestly, no, I'm not. I think Reissa feels I ought to be, and maybe you do too. Don't put Reissa's worries on me. Ever since you two have been seeing each other, he's been overly critical of me to the point of paranoia. I don't think our consulting partnership will work right now. Susanna, we aren't teenagers. We don't need a soap opera here. Life moves on and we are all doing well. You and I hold no animosity even if there are feelings or worries."

"Alright. I don't know, Jack. I'm just checking. We always said we weren't against each other and we're not. But, this is quite an adjustment. Sometimes you seem to be drifting and then again I'm not completely certain where I'm going. Me and Reissa, well, we'll see how it goes. So far, so good."

She stopped and looked around, changing the subject. "So, how's it working with that girl,

Molly?" She moved to get the tea, added a little cream.

"Not so good. She won't have anything to do with me. What can I say? I think she finds me odd, old, and needy." He sighed, looked down and towards the window. "I like her a lot. She's a beautiful delightful girl, fun, but there is something just not working. Besides, there's a whole world out there." He took a sip of the warm tea. Settled, he remembered the tea ritual he used to do when he was about 12. His family lived in an old 19th century stone house in rural New Jersey outside of Princeton. It was large and originally built to house debtors and other impoverished people. Sort of a 19th century version of workfare. It was called the Poor Farm and they lived on Poor Farm Road. He loved that place – large terraced fields surrounded by round tall wooded hills, his own bedroom, in a quiet valley. The place was special, but about two years ago when his parents got too old to take care of it and no one had the money to buy it, it was sold. To him, it was a failing not to have bought it himself. Quite a loss. It moved on.

The tea ritual in the old country kitchen, the fireplace, pine wood floors, … it was exhilarating in its own way. He'd take a Lipton tea bag and place it in a cup of boiling water. Then, against the hot stove he'd light fire to the paper wrapping and twirl it quickly until the paper was burned completely down. Because he twirled it, the moving air kept the heat away and it didn't burn his fingers. When it was almost gone, he knew the tea was ready. He'd take the bag out, drop it in the trash and put a little milk in the hot tea.

He faced Susanna, her head slightly tilted, looking at the floor, tea cup in her right hand dangling, a splash of tea left. "You know Susanna, I worry about you too; but then again, I don't. I ...." Before Jack could finish, Susanna looked up, paused, and said, "Jack, I still care about you. You know that, and I think we did well together. I'll always cherish that. It's just that I, you know ...." She stopped and looked away. "I can't let myself get stuck again. I like my life now. I like being more independent." She paused and stroked her hands. "Let's agree to take this new shot at life."

"Yes, I get that." Jack looked startled and paused before saying, "Do you understand? I wouldn't worry Susanna. And certainly not about us, or Reissa for that matter. You're getting stuck, or not, is your business not ours. If you're worried about Reissa, don't. He's going through his own self-evaluation. Just enjoy yourself and do what you have to do. We're all friends and can survive. It's about more than survival. We all seem to have come to a place in our lives where we want to be honest about what fulfills us and what is truthful. To not just accept the same old things without examining why." Here he stopped and added, "I accept myself. I accept you, Susanna; and I appreciate our time together. And, yes, sometimes I think it wasn't the right thing to separate. I really do. Still, I admire your courage to follow what moves you and that is inspiring. In fact, it keeps me going. We have always talked about that and we have a promise to support each other having a great life. Let's remember that, even if things seem a little odd or uncomfortable. I agree, let's be supportive. Let's take another shot at life."

Susanna left the kitchen and fetched a cup of tea; she poured a dash of milk in it and handed it to Jack who took one sip. Looking for a place to put it down, he placed it on the edge of a carved maple tea table. The antique with six baluster shaped legs and stretchers that he'd bought at a flea market in New Jersey about ten years ago. "Easy come, easy go."

Susanna lurched, "Oh Jack. Not there. Here." She thrust a piece of paper at him. "Put something underneath it. Shit!"

"Oh sorry. Yes." Jacks grabbed the paper, lifted the teacup and wiped the spot slowly.

Susanna frantically pushed Jack's attempts away. Trailing into a swish of napkin envy, toil and struggle, she got a wash cloth to clean it. But a little round steam mark hesitated where the teacup sat. Jack sat back in the sofa. The teacup poised like a small prince in his hand, its crown of steam a wave with whimsy, enjoying its human toys in consternation. "What, me worry?'

Jack took a check out of his coat pocket and placed it where the tea cup was, and smiled at Susanna who is standing next to him. She stared at it a second, then touched the check and picked it up. She turned around and took a sip of tea from a delicate cup that Jack recognizes was from their wedding china pattern collection. Her back is turned away from Jack; her long Kimono is red, gold, green and black with embroidered trim that swirls in puffs just above the floor.

Jack got up and took a step towards her. His right hand nervously touched his forehead and trailed above his temple to lightly touch the crown of his head three times as if to scratch an itch. He hesitated, then put his hand on her shoulder. Her chin dropped slightly and a teasteam dervish danced up her jawline, settled past her cheek, and stayed there like an angel's hand. She felt Jack hold her waist and move behind her. As his hand moved from hip to belly, he pressed at her navel and drew her to her place. She held the warm teacup with two hands in front of her face.

She spoke into her tea, "I have a chance to go to Paris on a fellowship for three months. I'm going to apply. It could help me get a job back here as curator at the Museum of Modern Art."

"If you go to Paris that long, what about you and Reissa?" Jack asked, with exaggerated skepticism.

"You're right. Reissa has his own life. You know I'm fond of him, but he isn't my boyfriend." Jack wasn't surprised by this statement. "And, this is a great opportunity to study and travel." She hesitated, "By the way, are you coming to my party Friday night?"

Jack laughed, "If it's anything like last year's, I wouldn't miss it."

He heard the alto voice recite a short poem.

they linger
where a wink
would stay the course much better

GIBBON MOON

The sunset bursts across the late November sky with a dangerous jagged lust. Every eye is held to dwell with another. Each want must wait for a mate. In different times, in different places on an earth unknown and charged with desertion, each attraction stays alive. A bruised sky beats back a gibbon moon. This moon laps a tongue of brilliant whiteness on that sunset hang dog yawn, a falling poppled peach, its bobbing presence buttock pale. In Riverside Park, Jack in a dark green wool winter knee length coat walked on the path by the river, stared across the horizon and up at a faint, almost full moon; and his thoughts flickered.

when we set out
to escape into a place less known
less beaten
when we follow an urge to slip away
drenched in raw plain skin
there is a void to be filled

in this void tumbles a sweet touch
felt and pondered
soft and silk gentle

can you feel a tongue warm layered
like a bough against the tide of swelling lift?
dwelling across arching hips
that speak nakedness
brandied in a swim of potent whimsy
to surrender what is owned inside
given when attracted by an invitation

when we listen
we might find a pear, a peach and barley
in the whimper
that is placed beside our beds at night, and
told to us sincerely
"if only"
this does not feel like love
in tongues of plenty
it feels like an ebbing tide
in its own peculiar necessaries it pursues what it needs
those tongues say what they may
and dance where they might

A rip of tongue red against the sky swollen in an indigo fatigue of lassie behind a welting yelp and wet look. Jack looked up at the airplanes overhead. Airplanes sperm across the sky to land in Newark and LaGuardia airports, and others shift the heavens with a load of sappy lick. People bunched together up there, sitting together, chairs in the sky. Maybe one fellow places a palm across a lady's thigh en route to Frankfurt; maybe, slipping as the knees take flight. Does she respond and cruise her mouth to linger by his ear? Does she move closer and press his shoulder to her chest as indigo gives way to deeper and deeper blues? "Of course. Indeed. Indubitably. That is, ... no doubt."

Jack noticed that the gibbon moon seemed to drift as clouds passed by. Its back bent in shame and shyness. The night will place seriousness aside and flatter the entire world with gibbon torch and generosity. The honey suckle droop of shyness from behind. It says, "I feel your care, your love." Inevitable as luck is when bounty brings a bitter laugh. The moon almost full, wanting, waits as beauty bears a pear on slender branch in the weighted part of years.

Jack stood on the pier at dusk and ate a Hershey's chocolate almond bar. Airplanes were flying south above New Jersey. Trawlers cruised up the Hudson River for an evening docking. Tugboats would take them back at dawn. He remembered the pang of loneliness he'd felt after leaving Susanna that morning. "Let it go."

THE PARTY

The past week was spectacular. Mountains of splashing sun and whipples of fresh cool December air lingered. The kind of air that can freeze beauty in a moment so that every glimpse is perfect. The cool air and a good wool coat is a tarp of radiant heat. If you're lucky enough to hold someone and slip your hands inside their coat, it's a mutual warmth, mammal warmth.

"It occurs to me," thought Jack, "that being a mammal is a unique form of consciousness, a conscious affection. Tantalizing shared generating warmths. Mammals do that well. There's something very provocative in that heat-generating, heat-seeking presentation. Maybe a mammal's greatest sense is their sense of warmth. Eyesight, smell, intuition, reason way down the ladder of perception. All are servants to this sense of warmth, alchemizing the kinetic into the telekinetic ... and giving the mind a place to dwell."

Jack attempted another call to Molly. She didn't answer and he left a message, "Call me." The call was not returned.

A burning rip of ginger bunt filled Molly's hands as she settled down on the green cushioned sofa in her living room. She sipped Chardonnay and crunched macadamias with suck and bite, dwelling on the billied holler of Jack's plea. Thoughts of dandy warmth, grizzled light, and a battled mammal pulse drew great against her hips. She pressed those eager hands along a familiar and furrowed mix. She touched and pinched velvet, her nipple in a sweat until the cushion felt the burrow of her dance. There was purr within the furtive maw.

Susanna's 35th birthday party surged until the wee hours. A swinging downtown atomic tribalism of rapture, giddiness, and the kind of delightful despair that could only be quelled when the end of the party drew nearer and nearer to the coming dawn. Susanna always threw a good party for herself.

Susanna looked ravishing in a long shoulder less burgundy gown, earrings queeny bridal sacred drip. A splendid sacrifice of skin. Soft and sweet, this mortal manna returned to be a tender dish for an eternal chew. Another splendid lady skipped across the dance floor and grabbed Susanna with a blushing embrace causing an explosion of dance. The dance floor humped and groaned with the grateful silos of urban rhythmed shuffle.

Susanna, master of the come-hither look, reached to integrate her life and her tribes. She melted within a cascading reach of friends, family, lovers all in one place at one time. They acted badly and that's OK with Susanna. "Naughty zazzed imps, cloven hoofed, wine splashing fools," Jack gurgled between sips of a shakier Bombay martini to someone in a light blue pirates outfit, feathered hat and all. Hushed in the corners, whispers rising like dough, growling between feedings of rich deep chocolate cake. They danced the funky Broadway, dipping in for the grind. At least nothing caught on fire, no one pulled the alarm, and if they had, they'd dance through it. Women and men danced in leaps and tantrumed weeping embrace. Bosoms flounce and bodies hush up close until the risk of impartiality withdrew. They fell into each other's arms rising in thick and breathy stares.

In the pre-dawn before the party dimmed, Jack looked around the room and saw a lone shoe down the hall in front of the coat closet. He mused, "A high-heeled ladies footed wrap lay there sideways. Fallen on the floor, a dazed and fobbed lilt pittoon bip drop ... a whiff of rush and drop. But, it's not the bother of the shoe that anyone would worry about. It's just a dance shoe flipped, dipped, and lost at whim to wangle in cornered serendipity. Was the lady lost or was the shoe? Or had she found someone who found the shoe a nuisance?"

The shoe lay on its side, askew in silent knowledge of the dropping hem. Dropped when midnight gave a chance to duck away. But quack, this shoe could not. If fabled air went flush from chest to tongue, this shoe could only beg in vain. For comfort, in the lady's graceful plan, was to depart from it abruptly. Her foot was free and warm in the dancer's hand, after tango tarted twists stretched the leather loose. She tossed the shoe like trash and found the tryst a better fit."

Jack emailed Gabriella: "Hey gorgeous, Just got back from a decent party, a birthday party with some wine splashin' fools. What's happening at your end of town?"

ARROGANCE IN A WORLD GONE SLIGHTLY MAD

Jack finished a supper of chicken noodle soup and toast with almond butter. Thanksgiving with family in New Jersey was great. Wonderful, really. When he got on the train back to New York City, around 3pm, his father shook his hand, then gave him a quick hug, saying "It's good to see you." Jack brought him up to speed with his divorce. "We both are doing well." Then he said to his father, "I found this very nice lady. Her name is Gabriella." They talked and his father ended by putting his hand on Jack's shoulder, saying, "Remember, be affectionate; even if you have to force yourself."

When Jack got back to his apartment in Manhattan, it was just before 5pm. He hung up his warm dark olive green wool overcoat in the closet in the small foyer area to the left just as you walked through the apartment doors. He walked a few steps from the foyer to the larger living room, where all the walls were painted off-china white in the old pre-war building. The dining table area was off to the left around the corner; He used the table as a desk, where his computer, an old friend, a confidant, waited obediently. He leaned over the table and pushed the computer's on button. The small green light on the top popped and smiled brightly; so did the little red light on the screen. Then the screen said "hello" as if to merge, to merge with him effortlessly, part of the routine, maybe get a cup of coffee and dance together. He noticed he'd received an email from Gabriella.

Gabriella: Jack, I was wondering how you are. How is the view out of your window? The sunset was lovely tonight.

Jack smiled and replied.

Jack: Yes, hello Gabriella. Happy Thanksgiving. Your email is just what I needed. I just got back from New Jersey, all the way out west. Let me look out the window.

He was feeling good, and this was very nice hearing from her. He walked over to the window and back to the computer.

Jack: Yes, you're correct. The sunset is lovely. It is lovely for everyone. You would think this is obvious, but I am certain it isn't. The moment humanity sees this (as a whole), will be the next stage in human evolution. Anyhow, it's great to hear from you. I didn't know if I'd hear from you.

Gabriella: Thank you. Of course you would hear from me. Tell me, how was Thanksgiving?

Jack: The whole week has had great weather, and it's been a particularly beautiful autumn day. It's my favorite kind of weather – crisp and sunny, cool but not cold. The rain let up on Monday and I spent Wednesday going downtown to galleries, then up to the Guggenheim. I walked back across the park at dusk and down along the river. Just walking in silence. It's quiet there at dusk. My folks came into the City from New Jersey yesterday about noon and we went to Radio City Music Hall to see the Christmas show. It was great. Then they drove us all across New Jersey to Stockton on the Delaware where we had Thanksgiving dinner at the Inn. There was no traffic; we literally got there in less than an hour. But, it's different. It's an old river town. If the town has 500 people, it would be a lot.

Gabriella: Sounds great. Why there. Why that Inn?

Jack: It's a great spot north of Trenton, south of Frenchtown. I grew up in that area, but a bit closer to Princeton. I stayed over at my parents' house last night. The transition coming home from that place, those people, to here is always for me like traveling across the ocean to a foreign place. It seems so separate, so far away.

I got home about a half-hour ago to my computer, some chicken soup, and of course, my guitar and books, the two pictures of ducks on the walls, and I'll go up on the roof of my building later. It has a wonderful and clear western view. I can imagine I'm looking at Stockton and across the continent. The roof is my microcosmic sanctuary. How was your holiday?

Gabriella: We can't get to the roof on my building. You're lucky. I had Thanksgiving with a few of my friends. I came home around 5pm and took a walk around the neighborhood. It was nice, quiet.

Sorry I took so long to call. I got caught up in what I'm doing. My work is picking up. So, what's going on with you?

Jack: I'm glad you reached out. Business is ok, but that's not what's on my mind. I'd like to share some of my thoughts with you. (He hesitates.)

Gabriella: Yes? Go ahead.

Jack: What I'm about to share with you may be a bit long and a bit odd. If it bothers you, say so.

Gabriella: Nothing's going to bother me unless you're writing a manifesto about the end of the world. And, that would only bother me if it was severely inhumane, or based on an invasion from outer space. Because, both have been done before.

Jack: No, it's not a manifesto and it's definitely not end of the world stuff. It's quite the opposite. This is what's going on for me. I was walking and thinking about the world we live in and how it works, and frankly, what it is to be a human being. Who am I? Who are we? I hope you don't mind my sending it to you as an attachment. It's a bit long. Let me know what you think.

THE ATTACHMENT

Jack sent the attachment in an email to Gabriella:

When I look at our world culture, I notice there is a great arrogance, particularly in what we call the civilized world. Our arrogance dwells in feelings of the certainty that survival is a matter of technology, and that we are superior in our capability. It is arrogant to think that technology is the height of civilization when the evidence is sharply to the contrary. I'm not saying technology is wrong. The belief of ownership over all things, that is arrogant to me. I'm afraid we will pay a steep price for it.

There is no reason why any person on this planet should live in fear of his or her basic survival. Changing our world attitude and systems to eliminate this fear is more than possible.

A world that worships fear is not something new. It has always been with us. And yet, there are clearly movements beyond fear that have also always been with us. These two forces have been in a struggle since consciousness emerged from unconscious. There is a struggle between the forces that integrate and those that separate. The emerging consciousness that values each tribe, each individual, humanity and the Earth as the only most important whole thing, is not fully integrated. In most of the world, the idea of integration is still not available even after being introduced thousands of years ago. For instance, this integrative potential allows each person to look into the eyes of another and see themselves fully. The separation that arises with fear is not political, but one of consciousness; separation being the inability to see ourselves in another. The consciousness capable of perceiving an integral world and manifesting this potential is not fully accessed yet; although I believe it is available to us.

Those who have reached this potential must teach others what value it is, and it seems they have. That is, a thorough teaching to people about what is valuable about them. This may seem easy, but the awareness of humanity is designed initially to look for simple exterior similarities akin to itself and to notice differences upon that palette. Integration occurs within. Even with our scientific knowledge of DNA and physics, which reveal integrative systems, we have not changed humanity's viewpoint that much. The reason is simple. Most people on the planet are not educated to these discoveries or their integrative implications, and have no access to this education. Those in the so-called civilized world forget this

– as long as they are able to get their premium cup of coffee each morning. But, I think things are changing.

Gabriella: Jack, I think that piece was beautifully expressed and there is truth to it. I don't usually meet someone who thinks like that.

Most people in the civilized world have almost no idea that a large number of people have virtually little of their basic survival needs met, and virtually no level of comfort allowing them to train and educate themselves. Therefore, they do not see the world the way you do. Not only because it is missing in them, but because they never get the chance. In many parts of the world, people are not docile; but are energetic and thinking people stymied by a world that does not work for them. And in most cases, and devalues them. When I look at humanity as a whole, I see this as the seed of all dismay and suffering. It points to a sad and unnecessary conversation of our humanity that each community harbors, even in the best of times and places. Look deep enough and there is an irrational fear in our hearts, and anxiousness about our very worthiness to be alive. Man's inhumanity to man seems to have no bounds.

Jack: Yes. This, I believe, is because we live in a world-consciousness that glorifies scarcity. We do so while in an ocean of endless possibility, justifying and glorifying our greed in piles of waste, demanding that other people feel our pain in the face of our selfishness, while talking in boring monologues to children deaf from starvation, compelled to listen with their last breath.

This is humanity as a whole today. It is a terrifying world worshipping a myth of scarcity. People are terrified there is not enough for everyone, and so there must be sacrifices. When we look truthfully into our thoughts of the world we live in, we see that we live in ignominious terror for our very survival and worth. We then trick ourselves with justifications, addictions, and compulsions. We are terrified of each other because of a neurotic, bordering on psychotic, sense of scarcity and loss, and with a repressed sense of abundance. Not just nations terrified of other nations, but brother against brother, parent against child, and friend against friend.

Gabriella: I agree. And we, that is, humanity, has known this forever. I think what you are saying is that it's what we do not know that will release us from fear. To change, we must change our perceptions and consciousness to be able to see abundance. To re-define what fulfillment in life is.

Jack: Exactly. And I believe this is happening, albeit at a slow pace and not in every sector at the same pace. We seem to live in a world where people are at varying degrees of awakening to this new consciousness, and some who already have awakened. Though people who have awakened more often than not come across as alien, and in conflict with older ways. Not until real survival is absolutely necessary will people close ranks, and then often, with trepidation. It is at these times, however, that transformation to an integrated human vision is possible.

Transformation to abundance is ongoing. Our children inherit the same world we did with the same choice and mission: to wake up to abundance ... or not. Waking up requires learning how to use new tools of consciousness. These tools are held by the mind in language and the power to communicate. And so, they must be taught.

The greatest tool that can be developed is an inquiry into what is worthy, whole, and complete for everyone. If we teach our children to dedicate their lives to this inquiry, their lives will be fulfilled beautifully. The second greatest tool is honor. That is the ability to live honorably, to acknowledge that which is good. The third greatest tool is honesty or truth. This is the ability to embrace life and accept reality as it is, and not as a dream. It has been said that myths are public dreams; dreams are private myths. A myth is never the end of an inquiry. Teach children these tools and they may change the world forever, and face fear with dignity and purpose.

Gabriella: Jack, thanks for sending me that. I can honestly say I've felt about things in much the same way.

Jack: Thanks sweetheart; I appreciate that. I don't always get that response. (There's a short beckoning silence.)

I'd like to see you again, soon. How about the following Monday night, eight days from today? I know a great Italian Restaurant in the Theatre District. Cozy, the food is great. By the way, I never got your last name.

Gabriella: Yes, absolutely. My last name is Picasso, like the painter. Monday is good for me. Let me know where it is and I'll meet you at 7 pm. I can't wait. That's December 7th.

Jack: Yes, the 7th. (He pauses ...)

Gabriella, you know, a lot of what I wrote I sort of hear first in my head as if voices are speaking to me. I mean real voices. It started happening early this year. Do you find that odd?

Gabriella: They're guides, Jack. Like spiritual guides, counselors. I've heard about this. Pay attention to them, write it down. It's ok.

111

THE MELTING PROMISE

Jack called Gabriella. They met for dinner at Rovero's, a midtown Italian restaurant on West 45ᵗʰ Street, Restaurant Row. They ordered a ragout of eggplant, zucchini, and an array of garlicked gastronometry. Plus, ricotta mixed with spinach, pureed and wrapped in semolina, delicacies in garlic and olive oil.

"Pasta dipped in slow melt tomato-olive-oiled sensuality. Tasty melt of peppered cheese and leaf Brazilian boppo. Risotto angel of god sipped unctuous drip and melt in hollow mouthful scream. Sipping wine with hints of cherried plum and malted lappenal din. Baby length gasps of delight, lisping furtive foundlings. We find the ship of wink and wade in." Jack played with these descriptions, thinking of them against jazz piano riffs. He listened to an interrupting sound bite from one of his guides. That's what Gabriella called the voices, guides. But, this voice is not the male; it is the sensual female alto voice.

"She has a heart of gold, and spicy wounded feminine eyes."

Jack enjoyed Gabriella. He looked into her mysterious full sparkling chocolate eyes and thought, *"She is beautiful."* He said aloud, "I enjoy your company. Thank you." A poem ran forth.

your joy is my bliss
your sweetness my weakness
your touch is my heart
your fears are my courage
when we touch
think of the gentle heart
in your whispering soul
and my hands holding your waist
just the way you like it

"Jack," Gabriella leaned across the table and cradled his chin in her soft left hand, "I like you."

He leaned towards her, "I like you too." He kissed her soft and sure, and then again much longer. And, the poem continued.

I wish for you
with a kiss rubious and ruffed
with vanilla and chocolate syrup
and a cup of nutty burnt bean joe

"Tender toes beneath the Florentine tableau." Jack's silent inner voice slipped past a sip of wine and beyond Jack's gaze, "I sense an offer." And then, Jack heard the male guide's voice softly say, *"a promise, a promise is tingling as emerging adoration."*

"You are lovely Gabriella. Adorable."

"Thank you, Jack. I find you to be a breath of fresh air."

Fragrant beanery melted into a delicious brew ... flan arrived with coffee and wiggles. Again, Jack heard the soft voice speak to him.

"A promise of authenticity, of real need and ease to share, is quite an invitation. If noticed for what it is not, there is a chance of a real promise to what it is. Be gentle with the simplest awakenings."

A late dinner, Molly ordered a pizza and a half-hour later, she buzzed the delivery boy up. "Knock. Knock." A peppered pizza boy delivered late and lingered.

Slip of gaggled gal gave boy a giggle. Tasted pizza, an urge to lick salt water in tangled twist of hoppy. Her dress was pulled up, flounced around her waist, and knicked kicked flippy shoe sailed bat-like across the wedded room. His waist went tight against her belly such that light is madness in the griddle of this darkened rush. Seems hesitation was less intent on fatherhood than boy be damned. His decadent back arched mighty in the haste of her forgotten sass. Feathered hand alight with bang and grip on that boy's ass.

—⚬⚭⚮⚯—

"The Manhattan night is crisp and clear. The cold December evening with no wind stays fresh while atomic radiation burps stars ... in places like the Great Cloud Nebula. That is what I'm told. In time this is noticed by anecdotal jibber jaw and maw-maw in the curious innocence of happenstance and the repartee that gives each drama its meaning." Jack laughed at this thought as they walked home.

Gabriella asked, "What's so funny?"

Jack stopped and apologized, "Well, like I told you, I get these interesting thoughts, like voices, and I hear odd poetic descriptions of things. Some make sense. Some don't. It's as if my mind is trying out some new language, or new use of English. For instance, the phrase 'this is noticed by anecdotal jibber jaw and maw-maw' just came to me. Now, that's sort of odd, but the thing is, I know what it means. Maybe, I get too carried away with the scat."

"No, I like the scat," Gabriella added quickly. She giggled. "Yes, of course. It means that we only notice things when we talk about them. Even if it's just talking to ourselves or yakking away about something. But, that's a funny way to say it."

"When we've all said everything we've already always said, and nothing different has happened, do we just go back to our respective separate corners of the boxing ring and wait for the next bell and do it all over the same way again, or do we begin to learn to speak another language?" Jack replied. "That's what I think the voices are telling me."

"I think Wittgenstein said, 'Language is the house of being.'"

Jack smiled, "Yes, that's about what it means to me. It's kind of funny. What I was thinking about before that was why this all happens. How the whole Universe is happening all the time, and of course we can't know that. We can't know everything that's happening. Yet, everything that happens can affect us eventually. Even the most remote things like quasars. Somehow their energy can affect us. We sense it in some way and it changes our perspective. It offers us something new."

Gabriella turned towards Jack and puts her hands on his shoulders, looking him in the eye. "You've got an idiosyncratic mind, buddy," she said firmly, but with excitement. She had a huge smile and her eyes were sparkling. "And you know what?" she paused. Jack stood still, his brown and black silk fedora on, olive green wool coat that hung to his calves, and an apprehensive look on his face. She continued in a gentler voice, "I agree with you. I've thought about that a lot myself. It occurs to me that we may first sense changes in the Universe in our bones and that gives us information that we first get by feeling it. Our feelings and sensations are a form of intelligence. They trigger our minds to think about it and have us imagine things like that phrase 'jibber jaw and maw maw.' Maybe that's where all original ideas come from. From our bodies sensing subtle changes in the Universe. Maybe ideas are our way of understanding Kosmic occurrences and energy. The energy becomes ideas and the ideas, words; the words become conversations, and the conversations create reality. Maybe one of the key things we do is transform energy into ideas. That's a powerful reality. It makes sense to me."

"Yes, it's beginning to make a lot of sense to me too." Jack's shoulders dropped. He brought his hands up to hold her waist and her hands relaxed around his neck.

"Gabriella, I think you're right. I have guides, like spirit guides that actually talk to me."

"Like I told you. I've heard of that sort of thing. Tell me more about it."

Jack told her about his shamanic experience with Truman. "It's starting to change my perspective on life and what I'm up to. I've never really talked to anyone about this."

Gabriella smiled, "I understand. I really do. I would trust this Jack. And you can talk to me about it anytime. My advice is, trust it and see what happens. I'll help you with it."

GABRIELLA TUMBLES

Jack and Gabriella tumbled into an easy winter. While Jack was in San Francisco running a seminar with Reissa, Gabriella and Jack tripped along the telephonic bing and gracious remedy of electronics ensured via the internet where bodies float in seemingly harmless whiffs of causal energies by finger-tap and modem.

Jack called Gabriella, wallowing in erotic sambas. "I imagine sitting between your thighs and letting the river of your blessings niagara through my swimming joy."

Eventually he opened up to her, revealing memories and aspirations not spoken of for a while. Ideas and desires that seemed stuck in the pockets of his trousers, laden with the pollen of coinage unspent. A breath of barter, touched with swoon and vigor, brought them closer. Passion erupted in their choice of destiny with a fluttering heart. Jack emailed and wrote of "shameless nipples budding to a lip-rent mist." This sounded right to her, and so she wrote him back; and he pursued her through the beginning of winter.

Jack emailed: I will bathe you when I see you. We will get flowers and fruit, and put them in the warm bath and let you soak. I will bring fine soap and mix it with honey and spices, and wash you, and light candles and incense and let you know your beauty.

Gabriella: I could read this over and over again. I feel so comforted, soft, loved, cared for. I wish you were here right now.

Jack: I could swear I know you from some other place in my life. I know that is mysterious and improvable. Last night, I had this tremendous feeling and saw a blue-white energy force/light exploding out of my body. I sensed that we are sourcing some powerful force that is transforming me and maybe you as well. This is no simple love.

Gabriella: I felt your presence at about 3pm today. You came in strong.

Jack: The energy between us is so loving and sensual. I am amazed that I have found someone like this. And yes, I had a moment today of "is this true?" I am turned on by the woman you are. You have the best female energy. I would venture to say we both have been seeking each other.

Gabriella: I agree. I have been aware for some time that there is intelligence to attraction that is deeply spiritual and necessary for awakening. Meeting you is not an accidental relationship. Feeling attracted is the essential energy. It means we are connected and the chakras are turning. I love your honesty and sensual intelligence. What happened last night? Did you think of me last night?

Jack: Yes, and I sent you very deep energy and saw myself holding your naked waist and gentle belly. You seemed so gentle with your nakedness, like a light breeze. And, if I could have just touched your lips when you whispered at the end of our conversation on the phone last night, I would have done anything to be there in that moment. I can't wait to see you again.

"I've finally met the person I've been looking for," Jack whispered in her ear on New Year's Eve.

Gabriella held him close. She smelled the wicked yearn and spice about his neck, and in her thoughts she heard herself say, "He is the one."

Jack looked into her eyes and a quick alto voice spoke to him, *"Yes. Say yes. I will. Yes, and again Yes."*

"Is that James Joyce?" Jack wonders.

ATOMIC ORIGINS

—◦⊸⊸⊸◦—

"Peppered beat and sullied sal boo-troon snaps beetle lady whiffet from bar stool to bar stool. Ground gravy murking squeal sets hip against a swiveled grind of turn." Jack listened to the antics of his imagination, had a sip of beer, and noticed Gabriella approaching. "Patterned slink brings belly up for pat and slips his hand beneath her sweater. She feels him advance in tender grip."

—◦⊸⊸⊸◦—

Reissa walked down 2nd Ave. He was happy to be back from California. He saw a beggar with brilliant eyes gone dharma in the depth of substance snickers when the dime did a jingle dance in Styrofoam. Reissa looked at him and held the beggar's ancient gaze, and sought a place to clear his mind of trash, and tangle. But the eyes were full of emptiness that had no trash.

—◦⊸⊸⊸◦—

Molly walked across 42nd Street at Times Square wearing a mustard yellow ski jacket, her favorite red fuzzy sweater over a black turtle neck, a bright shamanic scarf with red and yellow tassels, knee-high black boots and black leather pants gone mad with welts on the curve of purposeful lament. She licked her lips and ate a cheeseburger while watching the tickertape flash news that whips up a sort of insant-ania of world events. It disappeared as soon as it arrived.

Later at Gabriella's apartment, Jack whispered, "Gabriella" into her wash of dark chestnut curled whimsy. A soft gush gathered flush of rose pink and royal blue fainting sheen-of-light was around her cresting cheeks. "As the body moves through the soul, so does the world through her spicy wounded feminine eyes," he heard himself say. "Tender with a waiting gaze upon the look of gift." He stayed the night, and early in the morning just after daybreak, he headed back home while Gabriella slept.

The next morning in the beat of 9am, Gabriella rested in bed, covers pulled up to her chin. The watery gray blue sun sent waiting effervescence through her bedroom window. It dallied across the foot of her bed and settled in the corners of her womb and on the articles of her domain. Raw white wool sweater draped like a sad child called in from play hung over a wooden chair that stood sentry to whomever would seek its settled throne. She pulled her arms between her breasts and the breath of her lover dwelled between her legs. A reminder of his trip as he sought the fertile lay of her lost and full thighs, and warmed her hips with panthered tramp and toil. This brought a sigh that turned the blue to rosy red. It bent the filtered light to yellow-blue atomic in its origins. And here, the covers were a friend. They gathered sounds and stroked an infrared dwell held by woman. There was precious time to linger longer. The sweater waited with envy. Her cat slipped into the room to purr and lick the salty air.

Jack walked home with questions on his mind. He stopped for a cup of coffee at an all night Tribeca diner, The Silver Moon. "A craggy bloom of desolation. Why is he here in such a deadpan hush? Sitting with broken transverse matey slugs, with sycophantic whip of trouser ghost gone wavy. Who would wish to wake up in this murgatroid and eat here alone?" said the inner voice. "Why did I leave her so early?" He ate slowly. His brow creased against an awakened horizon while a zaftig she-bane Sargasso Sea awaited its dawn.

SARGASSO SEA

Later that morning Jack called and left a message on Gabriella's telephone. "Hi sweetheart. I hope your day is wonderful. Mine is. Sorry I had to leave so early. I had work to do. But, have you on my mind. I especially remember kissing you gently on your neck and lingering there to soak in your deliciousness."

As Gabriella walked down the hallway, a flush of Sunday light beamed in as she stopped, knelt and pets her cat who tilted her head up and purred. Her hair drying slowly after a long warm shower, brushed lightly against her knee and swept her breast with a lisp. She felt the spring-drift breath of Jack hover and wash the hush and open plums. She remembered him on her breasts full-mouthed and slow with a tugging pull. Tongue press lick tempered the nipples, and her womb wept. The flush of his cheek against her was gentle, his eyes closed and lost. She leaned over and kissed his forehead and he snuggled in closer in a wakeful dream. The sea of her embrace had no horizon and no place, crafting a timeless hum in the belly of a cradled wink.

THE ACHE OF TIME

If I touched my sweet tongue
to blushing breasts
point and proud
and eyes towards heaven
and then the cloven dance
alas gasp
I would only have
a memory of that taste
and if I pressed my body deep
within and about playful
sallied hips
while lost in those spicy wounded feminine eyes
I might only sense my fate
gone howling 'bout tomorrow's testimonials

and if I touched with envy
and brought the station of my hand
to rest in a muttered plastic moan
and whippet tell of crease and valley
and the crush of fruit wet lick
I might only be a craftsman of my death
done brittle in each fantastic allegory
a song that skin would tell

Susanned[?] in a tricky conspiracy
of fondly once I was

and so, I do not take your smile lightly
in our best departing
the best of scented mockery
a basil sweat mélange
sits tidy trussed
a tidy brew
bottled only by the ache of time

"Blushing breasts. Jesus! Jack, isn't that a bit sentimental even for you? Looking over Jack's shoulder as he finished the poem, Susanna spat with mock envy between a bite of pear.

Jack ignored her and emailed the poem to Gabriella. "You think Reissa will like this poem?" he turned and asked Susanna.

"Are you kidding? He'll think you've gone goofy, which I think you have!" Susanna said with an exasperated sigh. "What do you expect?"

"Okay, so you came over here to be a critic?" He sent the poem to Reissa.

Susanna huffed, "You know, he doesn't understand that sort of thing."

"You know Susanna, it's okay to let people know how you feel. Truth is, Gabriella is something else. I really like her and haven't felt this way in a long time. Our marriage may have broken up, but I absolutely believe in partnerships. This one looks very good."

"Hey! Don't get so defensive Jack. I'm just teasing you. Actually it's not such a bad poem. By the way, I believe in partnerships too, they come in many ways. But it's important to be in the right one. In some ways, you and I have a better partnership because we have a better friendship." She sighed. "I'm not sure exactly what I want in a partner yet, but when I do, you'll be the first to know." She sat on the sofa. "So, are you going to help me with my taxes or what?"

"Yes, of course. But, I'm not sure if I'm ready yet. I mean, having another serious relationship. I miss being married. I'm afraid I might not be able to make that happen again. What if I'm wrong about her?"

Susanna came over to Jack, "Listen Jack. There's nothing wrong with you. I've got things to find out about in my life, and you, well, you are different. As your wife, I couldn't support that so much. After you came back from that trip to Maine you were different, more focused but distant, farther along with your ideas. You need someone who can hear you and support you better than me.

This woman, Gabriella, sounds pretty damn good to me. Follow your heart and I'll follow mine. I'll support you about that."

She kissed him on the cheek. He shook his head up and down in agreement.

NARCISSUS

Reissa rapped his knuckles against wooden desk and popped his cheeks while glaring at his computer screen gone flush sky blue. A ticking indicator bleep patiently hobbed a call, a yearning moonbeam call, a dare. Jack's email came up.

Reissa wrote back quickly, "Jack, where the hell are you? What is this crap about 'spicy wounded feminine eyes?' What is this bullshit? What are you hiding from now? All your nice stuff again. It sounds off to me."

The sun shone through Jack's kitchen window, a winter sun blazing hard against his back almost burned him as he typed.

Jack chuckled and responded to Reissa, "Are you crazy or on drugs? This is one of the most asinine things I've ever heard you say. Open up, be romantic. You're so annoyingly analytical sometimes. It's just a poem. Do you have anything good to say?"

Getting up, Jack poured water into a blue metal teapot and turned on the stove. The bright day was welcoming. He thought to himself, "What is Reissa so afraid of? Making a commitment to Susanna? ... probably. Doesn't he know that's not necessary?"

"The sushi chop-chop and brittle bag of street life thinks nothing about shifting lives and opatata eek and pissle thwart poems." Jack heard this thought mixed with outside urban noise, car alarms, an ambulance siren in the distance, and cars rushing down the avenues. His thoughts drifted to Gabriella and a poem he started that morning.

—◦◦◦◦◦—

Shaded by the blush of time's determination
bathed in the wash of furtive passion
bent by love's last wish
like a cypress against the Grecian wind
waiting with a longing sunrise bashful whisper
she holds her lover with her crazy heart
and plays the blanket of her womb
against his able caress

and empties a fertile orchard of contentment
from prayerful breasts
and hips that tease a Kosmos song
sung at love's beginning
accepting the gingered bounty of life itself
In a fitful bowing release
man waits

—⟨⟨⟨⟨⟨⟨⟨⟨⟨⟨——

Jack saw a faint but clear reflection of his face in his kitchen window. Going over to his computer he wrote an email, but he couldn't think of whom to send it to.

I have fallen in love with Gabriella. Is it falling in love with mySELF? With some clear penetrating reflection of mySELF? Like the mirrors in my friend's lobby that face each other, the reflection is endlessly endless, back and forth in time and space to the infintisimal end. If I can and do step through that looking glass?

Then again, maybe it's all endorphins? Someone once asked me if love and passion endorphins existed. Of course. I can attest to that. It is a physically felt phenomenon like being tickled a lot. I don't know if I ache for the pain or the pleasure or both when she is not around. I'm here wondering if the human body or the "glue" that holds it all together is well built for this sort of thing. Even though I do not doubt the greeting of love's great reflection, I get to my "fear" of trusting myself. My ability to weather the storms of my own annihilation. That urge to no longer be only-me. At some point the reflection is transversed, passed through. What I see in my mind's eye is that the body will survive the transmutation and the inner SELF. The house of intentions, the residence of my beginnings has expanded and more rooms are lit. Something like this is happening with her and me.

"Damn! If Reissa read this, he'd go insane, ... again," Jack mumbled as he printed it out and took it from the printer. He filed it away and wrote another email to Reissa.

Email to Reissa:

Reissa, I thought the training in San Francisco went well. This month is shaping up as quite an exploration. New people continue to enter my life. New opportunities emerge. The money flows in interesting ways. And yet, I seem to be in a half-fatigue state. The morphogenic field murmurs, *"I am here ... old boy."*

He reads the email and realizes it will torture Reissa's sensibilities again, but in a good way. He continued.

Love in its purist state canters to the windowsill of my latent hope and I am cured except in my own dwelling where there is a vigilant lighthouse of fare-thee-well and follow-me-no-further. Yet, I have come this far to let go. To let a wish pass by my open hands and tug me into the next moment as easy as the evening tide. There is no shadow waiting, but a silent bruise that ties the heart to nature's calling, or was it an endless whisper from a twice-emerging star? In either case I'm thinking of Gabriella. We are getting along well, so take it easy on me.

Jack sent off the email and noticed a crumbled piece of paper by the trash can, a written halfling wonton, a burble scratch, a flif lying on the floor. It pleads pap, it prays incantationally. He sat for a few minutes and wrote.

Beauty sweet and born in cauldron brews
peaked spicy with a slight laced panty
so he speaks in hushed erotic reach
"you have the body for it"
and here a swoon meets swirling lip to bitten tongue
and there the bandy felt a whip of hipbone
merry 'tween thumb and index finger
and in that grasp is yet another whispered manacle
and in the leopard shimmy is a cry-gone femme

"Chance cannot change my love nor time impair," the voice said.

"Is that Robert Browning?" Jack wonders.

"Our innermost beings met and mixed."

FEBRUARY DROLL

Reissa reads Jack's email and feels annoyed. "Jack is moving on", he thinks out loud. "Does Susanna know? What happened to his interest in that girl, Molly? Well, she didn't seem that interested in Jack. Jack is just too serious for most people. But, Gabriella ...." This pissed him off.

He emailed Jack, "Not someone I noticed right away. Decent sort of gal, but a little standoffish. Distant, but unremarkable. From Northern Spain, I believe that's what she told me. A Basque maybe."

"She's Portuguese."

Susanna sat at her kitchen table. The February droll wept cold rain that stayed heavy and tired on the concrete sidewalks. The city seemed itching to get inside and wait for spring. Her apartment was warm and the light comforting. She held a neatly unfolded letter in her hand, a letter of acceptance from the museum on her fellowship. She went over her plans to go to Paris. Last year she'd met a

French photographer whom she was interested in. He had said to call if she was ever in Paris. Maybe he would give her a place to stay? Finding her red leather telephone book, she flipped through it, then reached for the phone and dialed Paris.

Her friend agreed to let her stay at his apartment. She emailed Reissa and copied it to Jack:

> My fellowship was accepted and I actually can leave within a week. I don't know why they waited until the last minute to tell me. Still, it's a great thing. I've been hoping to get this and continue researching in France. I'm going with about five people from Bard and the Smithsonian. You know, MOMA is interested in my work and I think I can get some kind of curator job with them when I get back. This trip will surely help. I'll be staying at a friend's apartment. I'm going to miss you. Can one of you give me a ride to the airport next Thursday? Wish me good luck.
>
> All my love,
> S

Jack read Susanna's email and wrote back, "Congratulations, Old Scream. I'm sorry, but I'm busy with a client that day." It's cold outside, but the sun was shining. He wrapped a heavy scarf around his neck and went for a walk.

LIFE'S ARISING STAGE

Jack walked down Broadway. Cragged in a sunset strip of derogatory burnt muse and paperized sexual zingers. On a bench in the meridian is an older man. The down and out sort wrapped and double wrapped in layers of neglected ware, clutching a paper coffee cup, a good graze of whitegray stubble, worn thrice work boots with the scrapes of wandering. The old man is engaged in an alcoholic wintry argument with a younger man possessed with fierce determination. The younger man, this kid, is draped in a black used navy wool pea coat, scraggly sweaters underneath, old blue jeans sagged about him, and beat up red Doc Marten boots over orange socks, a pull over red and blue wool cap obviously discovered in a lost and found box. Cigarette loafing on his lip, now and then he takes a drag by tilting his head up 20 degrees, squinting his eyes and inhaling seriously with inevitable scattered smoke and foggy breath. Jack walked by, stopped, and waiting for the traffic light to change, he overheard their conversation.

"No reprise for the wounded," the old Mugwump said to the nodus kid.

The kid let out a puff of smoke, smirked, and spit beatific, "But, what of a tight lipped panty grope blind side fuck-a-thon of hope for the situationally deprived? You know, those nymphomaniacled ethnic willow wisp and deep spread knee splayed tabernacle dreamed angel types, like us. What of those?" yelps the always adolescent. "The kind that dream of sports heroes and sex play in one complete thought and stage blissed out goo goo like gurus on a dharma line? What about those sort a folk? They're lost in the droxis."

They both burst out laughing, snorting, and coughing. "You're a crazy sumpin'-else," the old man chuckled and pulled a bottle from his coat and took a swig. Young man sang, "booley boolayyyyyyyyyyyyy," stood up and did an imitation of James Brown doing the shimmy at the Savoy. Sat down with a twist and stuck his cup out to a passerby. In plopped a few coins.

Jack was reminded of seals waiting out an Antarctic blizzard. This is what their conversations must sound like. *Ididectic logaodia.*

⸺⬯⬮⸻

Back home, Jack hunched over his kitchen table, a mug of French roast coffee in his right hand. Elbow on table, his left hand slapped a palm of murgatroid cross the sunset of his brow and he stared at the two small porcelain blue rabbit salt and pepper shakers on the table in front of the printer. His thoughts were buried in the depths of want and the taste of flesh that barters a bay of life's arisen stage and swells with a burst of seafoam wash. Washed wet on his palette brushed and humbled by a resistant ancient tide. And here, his own voice laps against a listening that dwells in perpetual annoyance that denies the purring hum of a woman's wanted knowledge – that here, and here alone, life begins and life does not lay fallow in fields of fidelity where only one hand may guide the till. Jack prepares himself for the battle of his existence, a known and marked man.

He bit his thumb and gnawed on the nail. "Has it come to this surrender?" Would he flee to the comfort of a jaded norm discarded on the table like leftovers at an all-day-all-you-can-eat buffet, each foot so simply and precisely stepped? He sips the coffee and pulls a slice of bread from its paper bag, places it in the toaster, and pushes down the on-button.

—◦◦◦—

If a slip of want
bit a narrow neck
blood filled
and full of breath,
would winter be less cold?

If a tongue rode the crevasse of your spine
and traveled up your neck
to sing at your napier
cragged in a sunset strip of derogatory burnt muse
and paper sexual zingers
Would the rip of your possessions be less battled?

And, if a promise
took a razored dagger and split your heart
and found a willingness to bleed,
Would you recognize the unfound day?
"'Tis better to ask for forgiveness"
she said and closed the light

The toast popped dark and crisp and Jack let it cool
a bit before buttering it with orange marmalade.
He wrote down the poem and emailed it to Reissa.
"'Tis better to ask for forgiveness," he muttered.

DELIGHT IN THE EAST

—⦿—

Gabriella faces the sun each morning and feels its essential warmth. Today she'll have three clients for energy sessions. As the months go on, she's become better known and now has many people seeking her, her touch floating in radiance. She prayed in a hushed but steady voice.

Earth and Sun.
I love you completely
great teachers
angels of light,
children of God.
I am an open vessel
that receives your love and light.
I fill my being
and overflow
with the joy
your love brings.
I send light and love
to heal everyone
on this earth
and helpers beyond.

She read a poem Jack had sent her that morning.

Shimmer and bliss of love
slip silent quick voice
touch the mind of grace
be thankful in your touch

new born each day
seek warmth
walk through winter
wander from ballied south
and return to boolie
when the sun sets higher
and from on high
its warmth is closer
and penetrates
go back home
go back and visit the past
speak with ancient whispers
delight in the east
the direction of courage and air
there is a new beginning rising
place a feather and float
always in the west
drop into the ocean
perhaps returning
having forged life from a keen bosom

Gabriella stood on the roof of Jack's apartment building in a long full satiny black dress, a rust colored wool shawl around her even shoulders. Eyes warm brown, secret and full of sky, clear and unexpected. High above the surrounding buildings – here, a clear view unobstructed to the north across the Hudson past the willo-of-audubon, glen ridge, and riverdale.

At noon Jack received an email from Reissa, "Yo, jerky. Cragged is <u>not</u> a verb, Jack. A crag is a rock."

Jack let the air out of his lungs slowly and wrote back, "Are you absolutely sure that's all there is to it, Reissa? Take a second and listen to the life of that word, feel its origins, its excitement to exist. You're a crag. I'm a crag. We get cragged being crags."

Reissa: Yeah, ok. You're just confusing people.

Jack: Maybe you're just confusing yourself. Language evolves. We need a new language if we want new things to happen. We constantly invent language with new words, new interpretations, and values placed on old words. You haven't noticed that?

Reissa: Why do we need a new language? What's the matter with the one we've got?

Jack: The fact is, it happens. The reason, I believe, we need new language is because who we are, who we experience ourselves as, is completely immersed in language. And, if we want to be different; if we want to grow, change, develop, obtain new levels of understanding, there must be something different about the language we traffic in. It must reveal new territory. Language designs different types of thinking, opens new capabilities and realities, and the ways we are conscious of the world around us. Through language, we are responsible for how the world occurs to us, how we operate in it, and how we perceive reality.

Reissa: Ok. So, where does new language come from?

Jack: It comes from all of us. It tells us who we are. It comes from existing language, and it comes from nothing. It arrives as our perceptions arise to name the reality we perceive. Maybe it comes from you today, maybe me tomorrow. New language isn't only inventing new words. New language is also the context of our conversations. The reality that holds the meaning of our words, the reality it invents. New language means something new to talk about. Language is always growing and trying to accommodate communication needs. As I see it, language can be said to be equivalent to consciousness, to what we are or are not conscious of, because it reflects who we are and what is real to us. Language manages consciousness. Consciousness looks like, walks like, and talks like the language we participate in. The thing is, are we aware that we invented this and can invent other realities, with new concepts, words, and new conversations? And the answer is, yes and no.

Reissa: That's how it is for you Jack. You never ask for permission, but you always want to be forgiven. Good luck with that.

With that, the email conversation ended. Jack stared at the screen. "That was an odd thing to say."

Jack wrote, "That's it?

No response.

―――――

ARCADIA

It was after 12 noon. Jack sat with his laptop computer on his lap. He'd been working for a week on a report about discourse analysis in decision-making and public policy. He got up and made a cucumber and bean sprout salad and heated up broccoli soup. Gabriella stopped by during a break from her clients.

"Are you OK?" She asked him.

"Yes, fine, just hanging around writing. I'm glad you stopped by. How's work?"

"It's picking up. Hey, I don't have much time; got to get back in a hour," she winks.

"We'll have some soup and salad first, Ok?"

Gabriella took Jack by the hand and walked him to the bedroom. A fly on the wall might have observed a loss of sock and lee. The door shut. If a barn might yell the passage of the sun that raises wheat through summer rain, and the floorboards tell a small mouse of a time once spent together in twilight forests where leaves drip rain patiently at dawn, then the walls of Jack's apartment might just keep their secrets.

An hour later, Jack again sat, computer pussied on his lap purring. Gabriella is gone. Lock brit and bane in a clippet finogram purposefully recording minutial torrents of Arcadia. The words stored and manipulated like the bacteria that feed on the detritus of earthworms, the manure of dust mites and protozoa. Without these little bastards, the kern of life would be even more desperately hungry than could be imagined by the pampered sycophantically vimpy dodgers dragged as they often are willy nilly to death's door. Jack digresses as the written word feasts on what could be forgotten and often should, but has its own life stored electronically, worked and reworked.

ROSEWATER COCOON

In the late night scheem jazzed nugatious fleen, a silent Molly combed her sassy hair and listened to Ellington. Humming snippets of urbane whim. Her tongue lingered in an open jocularity. Time's run out on the desperate datebook flaunt that had her hike a short black dress up to waist and tug the tarred nyloned leggings free to knee wait and accept a baffled happening hap long and cooled by winter. Buster lifted her knees, pressed them against his chest, and snarled gleefully into her dark eyes. She bit gently on his lips waiting on the edge of sham, a fluttering skirt buoyed by the extra swell her belly bartered.

A streak of rain swam the gravity of greased window and a perpetual hungry fog swallowed the lunar hour that Reissa knew as his shallow wait for Susanna. Mood indigo sung shadowed in appetizer munch and cocktail tease croons from his radio in the Manhattan East Side din below 14th Street. It must be strange when your wife doesn't come home. Even stranger when your friend's wife doesn't come home.

"The trouble with relationships," Reissa emailed Jack, "is recognizing the new pattern when the old pattern changes. Seems like only after things change can you notice these things. Is there any predictable reality in the Universe, let alone our relationships? At least not any that's knowable. Hindsight isn't knowing anything. By the time you recognize hindsight, it's too late. It's old news and confuses what's happening now."

Jack thought about this and responded, "The closest we will ever come to truth on this subject is to be honest about our delusions. I suppose that's the beginning of enlightenment, being honest about our delusions. All I feel we can hope for is to be a reflection of what is real. Is that good enough?"

Reissa wrote back, "Well, I guess it depends what you are a reflection of Jack. Am I giving you enough of a break?"

—◆◆◆—

Molly wiped away a tear and cleaned a stain of rouge in preparation for a night's sleep. She drew a warm wet cloth across her face, sprinkled it with rose water and, holding it gently to her nose, breathed in with a thankful smile.

ESCAPADE

Soft and spun, winter passed with a four-pack of Guinness nipped with a friend, a murmur and a snort. Dalliances lingering in the soft warm invitations kneaded with kick and rise. Waiting out the cold in civil obedience earned by grip and orchards gone from bitter to sweet. Fruit trees aimed to catch the monkey by the sweet tooth and keep 'em as a funny pet that chews the fruit and spreads the quiet seed in primate transmigrations. Bitter crunch to succulence. That's all it takes to hitch a ride with Gaia's jumping brains.

Susanna left for Paris last week with a group doing research at the Louvre. Reissa took her to the airport and later walked aimlessly around the East Village. He caught his reflection in a store window. "I need a haircut".

Susanna sipped tea at an outdoor café in Paris and watched a Frenchman kiss a dangling femme who settles like a summer leaf upon the sidewalk. She thought she heard him say, "tears and a half my love." But then again, her French was not that good. Held, cloistered in a romance of delicately chosen words laid secret by the Seine, where wine was sipped and her hand was raised and fingers brushed his brow. He hailed a cab to lift his sweetheart through the city, chatteled, mumphed, and murfted.

Reissa was thinking of how to re-design his consulting brochure, which he decided to title, *Moving with Excellence*. He has worked on it for five days and hardly left his apartment. Today, he took a walk, but not before he showered and washed some clothes.

Gabriella lay in bed and pulled a pillow closer, the one Jack slept on last night. She smelled the fit and wren of Jack's persistence. She dropped her head closer and muffled close the mane of want behind her bold and baffled breath.

Molly sighed on the periphery of droxis. It's almost spring.

———

Jack was on the roof and moved closer to the edge. Looked over, got dizzy, and walked away.

ON THE EDGE OF DROXIS

The light opens
on the edge of droxis

Two moths copulate
a-lot-a movement by the male

Under the hue born batoon slibble
is blue cheese norm knosh dribble and sit
and then there is the other keek of food
when flesh is eaten

The hair on her body is fine
at nexus a wisping froth
of tattum bundled shrubbery and bothered timber
dainty organum
twixt locomotion and ramboon

Thoughts of gentleness
baited by flight
and harbored past winter
in a silky white cocoon

She sleeps and wiggles
and glances fully
with a hither dither nom
elusive regretful fittery
is there joy in spring's
beckoned nappy?

Is there an almond-like taste
or sweet tea?
place pearl on tongue and teeth chew

Is the bashful flittering winged buzzer
an afterthought misplaced?
Or, just deadly?
a noetic miggle of wishwant and whimsy?
To place a seed in baleful blootin and begone

She pacifies a slipping sense of losery
chews a dense but easing flesh
and taps the same good humor to a sleeping mur
to awaken, caress,
and be brit and doggerel in the dannymore

A feral scent is apt to linger
an urge to cut away the cloth
so known and wrapped
and safe against the cold air
that surety
insists,
remains

JACK TURNS TO GABRIELLA

Gabriella and Jack walked the streets in SOHO just as the full moon pulled above the horizon.

Jack turned to Gabriella, "I'm hearing the voices, the guides."

Gabriella stared at him. Jack's head was bent slightly down and to the right. He's listening. "What are they saying?"

Jack stopped a moment, "Ok." He started walking, his right arm around her shoulder. She got close and they walked steady but slowly. "I'll say it just as they say it." Jack listened as they spoke. His voice seemed slightly different.

"Hope beckons often in the distortions of reality. When each look is a personal one. Each wish a jealous possessing clutch to battle the eel of loneliness where one might sell the empty side of the bed to a stranger who has the presence of mind to be warm. Who could blame anyone that dreads a fitful night seeped in only moonlight, or senseless in a stew of great great fear?

167

Who wants a twisted fate gone rotten with negligence and hesitation? Hope desires a clearer voice."

Jack turned to Gabriella and listened to an all too familiar call. Two voices spoke in an inquiry he had not heard 'til now.

Gabriella said, "Wait just a second, Jack. Let me record this." She fiddled with her handbag, dug in, and retrieved a small digital recording device.

"You carry a recorder with you?"

"I need it for my clients. To keep notes and various meditations, affirmations, and instructions. It can get detailed. My clients like getting the recordings. It helps them remember what we discussed."

Jack began to speak again and his voice modulated between low, deep male voice, and a higher pitched female voice, both slow and purposeful.

The lower voice, *"Life is an invitation. Think about these questions. What do we always say to each other? What has not been said?"*

The higher voice, *"The invitation. Also, what could we say?"* The voices alternate.

"A partnership. If standing at the edge of all that's been said. You are at the edge of droxis."

"Discovering what is possible. To say what has never been said before. Speak. Manifest."

He heard the male voice coming to him and in his mind's eye he saw the falcon jump the branch and fly towards the sea.

"Could there ever be two who'd meet and give a life so great that each would be a delivery of the other's purpose? Could it be that we would hold our greatness in the silence of another's ears? Would we trust the remnants of our souls to a brief and twilight flicker of recognition? We would if that opened the last and final gate of mystery, putting the imp of solitude to sea, ... wouldn't we?"

"I got that. Thanks," Gabriella smiled. "That was interesting. Let's do this. Let's record those voices again."

Jack smiled, "Sure. Thank you for listening."

THE TRAGEDY OF NOW

Bare in bone and step, Jack felt he was wandering through the zing of churning tarot to settle once again in his blue striped robe. His feet on the hardwood floor grew cold while witticism marched past a hearty call of fun. With zip and an urge to veer from the path of ancestral serfdom, Jack began his day. Not so much a complaint, Jack was determined to keep an arms length of annoyance alive in his pursuit of happiness. The shamanic voices had been more noticeable lately and began to show up in his dreams. He put the final touches on a training manual for a new client, then packed his bags to leave with Gabriella for a cabin on Indian Lake in the Adirondacks.

There is a gray-blue sheening glare
that blinds from dawn to noon
a late March glare
Gripped winter nippy, tight, begs for a bit of warmth
body to body and belly soft
Roast in front of timberal flame …

*crack–crack, drink wine
and eat together.*

Gabriella sat in a cozy chair with Jack, cuddled cling and rest in winter's waiting demise, tugged the warm snuff Zen from voluptuous wrap and bodies held tight. Undaunted by the traceable hum of root and planted hope, they kissed; and in that kiss, hormonal whim deepened life's great loss. The simple loss of ego where each moment passes all understanding. In their own peace, they merged. A tragedy of "I never was." The triumph of "We always are." Gently, Jack slipped his hand around Gabriella's silent waist and squeezed fullhand to give a little lift. She slipped a finger in his belly button and wiggled.

Jacks said to her, "Sweetheart, remember the voices I told you about, the ones that guide me?"

Snuggling in she said, "Of course. Have you been hearing them again?"

"Yes I have, and more so even in my dreams. They seem to approve of us. That is, I think they want to speak to both of us. What do think?" Jack held her close.

"Well yes, I feel drawn to them. I'd like to think they like us, or choose us. Don't you?"

"Yes I do," he said happily.

"Jack, from my experience, these guides are very special. I talk to a number of people with similar experiences. Most healers hear guides in some way or another. In your case, it's similar, but a little different. You're not just getting information, but instruction and philosophy. You have to trust your guides and trust yourself to listen to them. Give it a chance and you may be surprised by how much they want to be in contact with you." She looked at him intently.

"What do you mean?" He asked.

"I mean, it seems that although you listen to them, you aren't open to them completely. You treat them as some personal oddity rather than as a gift that you can share with others. If you open up to them as real entities you'll probably experience something extraordinary. Open up, trust them, give them a chance. Trust me on this one."

She paused, "Let's work together. When you hear them, tell me. I'll ask you to tell me what they say, and write it down. Just like the other night. Maybe, I'll get a chance to ask them some questions."

Jack heard, *A peace that passes all understanding.* He said, "Gabriella," holding onto the "l" like, "lllllll lllllllllllllllllllllllllllllllllll." ahhhh.

"Maybe," he whispered.

Winter passed in cradled crudités
dip and taste and wait

BLESSED SON –
BLESSED DAUGHTER

"Scrapo snarf blin of tuks," Jack's murmuring head lay against a swollen want as he awoke, whispered, and blithered, "If I taste I will want more, kiss you lightly but with a winking passion, there you go. But, are you counting the animus of life's less negotiated inclusions? Think not, but feel so much. How can such a lay of lips break the camel's back so swift? Is love a persistent betrayal as it flusters our first steps?" As Jack mumbled into his pillow, Gabriella rolled away and pulled the covers up to her chin. In his half-sleep, he heard the alto voice, mistaking it for her.

"It is the inner journey that finds a secret. When we touch our heart, we encounter our soul and it expands the edge of self. All else is a poor glance that never sees the true path where two become one, joyfully awaiting annihilation, and find that one less secret is the greater joy."

"That's beautiful sweetheart." He fell asleep.

At the breakfast table, Jack fumbled with a kitchen match to light a stick of Burmese incense and clear the air of nuon. The match juggled and played the sought-after burn. He snapped it firm against the bottom of his shoe and brought the raking flame to burn the stick. His face shined golden-red in the fire. His nose raked by the smoke, he sneezed. Gabriella laughed and Jack laughed too.

An hour later, the musty odor of sandalwood still clung to them as they walked through the woods along the lake shore. The leaves all spring-green flush and yellow-red, buds and blossoms full on trees and flowers, the wind blew through them with a bit of hesitation as he looked skyward to see the pregnant blue, and the voice of Gods hummed as blue might hum, *a blessed son, a blessed daughter.* They sat on a rock by a shallow stream that runs to the lake, and Gabriella took a sip of hot tea from a thermos. Jack took a sip; then, finding the recorder in her handbag, he lifted it to his lips and began to speak slowly, purposefully.

> *Ain't it great*
> *How we met?*
> *How we love and found love?*
> *and enjoy moments that last*
> *in a failed forever*
> *sought again and again*

I'm amazed at your heartfulness
towards me, made confident by
my willingness to bury my life
in the gentle grace of your lovely neck and
sweet femme lilt hair
We are now an essence unto ourselves
a vessel in a river of
tomorrow's fortune

Gabriella looked at Jack, smiled and laughed a sweet giggle. He leaned over and nipped her on the ear lobe. She protested, but not so much; and bit back all in tease and tempt and tipple.

REISSA REDUX

Dear Reissa:

So many thoughts of what I'm up to here. I'm spending more time wandering around the Tuileries Gardens alone this week. Wondering who I am and where I'm going rather than working on this research project.

I'm OK, but there is a real tension as to how to trust myself, or how to start letting go of not trusting. As if there is a "how." I think there is more sense in seeking what to do than how to do something. When I feel tight and unhappy, I look at my motivation for doing something. Is that motivation true to me now? Or, does it remind me of something past? Is it more a habitual response about what I think I ought to be or a response to what is actually occurring? Underneath it all, I feel I could be more forgiving of this tension before it becomes turmoil. I think this is how you and I might understand each other.

I try to be in the moment, but being in the world and living in the moment as a way of being is not always done. You can do it by removing yourself from the world like a monk or nun. It works but it is isolating, and it's not for everyone. Most people live in the world, with families, friends, and jobs. Being rounded and focused about our life's mission is often at odds with everyone else. It's not easy in the world, but it's exciting. It takes courage to be in the world and be aware. Running from place to place doesn't seem to create "the moment" any more than anything else. Although it is important to know ourselves and be honest about who we are, I think helping another seek their truth is a more powerful way to live.

On that note, I think about you often. Being with each other writing emails helps, but it is not like the warm touch or gentle look into your eyes. What is underneath it all for me is a fear of being alone. I suppose to some extent that is heavily charged with negative notions for you because I left so suddenly. I know often it is for me, as I anticipate suffering and loneliness. If you say I designed it that way, you're right. And so, accepting that need, I'll try to be gentler rather than stoic with myself. It's a choice.

Maybe I'll have a day of attention to myself, a day of kindness. Have a massage, paint my toenails, buy a good dessert, and things that I especially like. I might accept that my heart is vulnerable, but strong and purposeful, and that I enjoy life.

Life is magical if you think about it. We are designed to be with beauty. That's what Jack used to say. He said life is magical by its very existence. Noticing it existing is where goodness comes from. From the curve of our elbows to a shading of light at our feet. That we "see" this at all is magic. Noticing is joyful. Joy is power. Jack is right about that.

Anyhow, my work at the Louvre is going well. I'm staying with a friend, but I don't see him much. He's a workaholic, never around, and keeps the oddest hours. I'm starting to look forward to coming home.

All my love, Susanna

————

Dearest Susanna:

Sounds like you have time to think and that things are not so exciting over there. I haven't been working much lately. Maybe a few days a week or more. Most days, I stay in my apartment in Manhattan, maybe take a short walk through Tompkins Square Park. I enjoy that. I will slowly begin to work more, but I now feel detached. I have savings, but money is becoming an issue. I don't have much now and mostly feel compelled to "get some." But, I'm not so committed to that and don't want it to be my only reason for taking on more work again. That is: getting money. Because so much of that is, it's never enough anyway.

I am enjoying the time off. The great thing is, every week flows by. It also has a theme and often an invitation to meet and talk to someone, or design something new, or handle something. It's funny, life just occurs if you are open to it. But mostly, I admit I have this little crabby voice going on in my head, "I don't want to and you can't make me." So, I see that is a resistance and I don't know how to stop that, or even if it is necessary to stop it. The feeling that comes up is that I'm lost and want to be found. But not by some policing force. Not some "this is the way you must do or say things" force. That may be a reaction from working for twenty years in a corporation and being so good at being just that regimented force. Funny, I think I'm becoming more like Jack.

I don't know about anyone else, but when I look back, why did I take so long to get away and start consulting? I feel annoyed and ashamed of not going off on my own sooner. So often I

see that what I am "doing" is waiting for that
sense of shame to pass. I know it sounds stupid.

I miss you,
Love – Reissa

SAVAGE & SOUGHT

Pampered and snug by the Seine, by the Hudson, rivers of dreams, newly found laughter falls in night's late dark into the great wet and is slowly taken out to sea. Dinner for two plus two who finds whom? Strangers alerted through touch. The email follows. Here and there, each mystery host parlaying chance to taste life's sweetest waters. A play of attraction triggers mechanical, but its unknown in the mind's playroom where each desire is in itself a fantasy that makes promises from far away. What some might call the "other side," which is more and more a place that any life may bridge. Jack sat by the river and wrote.

If I could touch you with my quick tongue
I would fall into the swallow of your fertile breasts
My desire would burrow like seed beneath your
beating heart
and flower from the core of your born belly

There I would dwell apart from a
savage and seek roam

185

and pass gently past your home
and linger in soft weep and present squirm
to press my lips between our joy
and enter with a wish
veiled and cloven
who cries not from sadness or regret
but from a once and fraught greeting renewed with
a gingered kiss?

When would we not be us
if so returned and spun
such that a deepset moan is bailed in
a mouth that only hums?
Who returns this compliment without a smile?
Doesn't the river return the wet
of sky to deepest Ocean?
Yes.

THE HAIRDRESSER

Reissa stared out the window into the overcast afternoon. He was sitting at the hairdresser's waiting for his turn, wondering what Susanna might be doing in Paris.

A young lady came to him and told him she's ready. Her curly brown hair and slender body did not escape his notice. She took him to get his hair washed. He felt her fingers massage his scalp. It seemed so personal, so genuinely caring. She told him he has lovely hair. He smiled, eyes closed, as she rinsed his hair.

After wrapping a fluffy white towel around his head, she walked him to a firm-backed chair, covered in black vinyl. A round mirror in front, reflected scissors and lotions and dryers on a shelf under the mirror and Riessa noticed her smile as she looked at him. The light on him was bright but focused, giving a stage sense, an intimate interrogation.

She asked him what he does for a living. "A little management consulting," he replied. The conversation moved to music and nightlife. As she snipped the hair about his ears, a tingle went through him and he almost turned to kiss her cheek. When she shaped his eyebrows, she was so close he could feel her breath and smell a light ginger perfume on her gentle neck. She lingered. He opened his eyes. She stopped and her face lit up in a playful smile.

"What's your name?" asked Reissa.

Gently, in a slow giggle, she answered, "Molly;" and snipped at a piece of his eyebrow. Reissa admired her deep turquoise nail polish.

"Molly? I mean hello, nice to meet you, Molly."

"Glad to meet you." She paused with a quiz show hush, and Reissa stepped in as if on cue, "Reissa," he said quickly.

"Well, it's good to meet you, Reissa. Reissa, Reissa, Reissa," she rolled the name on her tongue, "what an interesting name." She pantomimed, "When you walked in, I could tell you were a man of distinction. A real big spender." She giggled, twisted her hips like Fosse, held her face close to his and smiled, her eyes dancing.

THE DEMAND

Sunny ease of 8am. Dulled by night sleep. An exterminator rang Jack's apartment buzzer to get in early and spritz the apartment with his wares. Just last night there was talk about insects. A silverfish was found in the bathtub. And, although this was not usual and there had been plumbing work done earlier in the week, which may have brought it on; it signaled a need to spray the place. Without much notice, the exterminator showed up first thing in the morning.

Jack drank his coffee and half of a toasted buttered bagel. Each morning had arrived with an edge this week. Almost an annoyance. Morning showed up like an annoying habit and other habits flowed forth. More coffee in the old white mug – unsweetened soymilk heated on the stove poured first, then the coffee for a perfect mix – twixt dew and dapple tern fuse muse.

Gabriella stayed the night; was sleeping late. This gave Jack time to be alone and to assess what needed to be done that day. Business calls, cleaning, dinner, writing, romance, meetings, conversations. Of all the things Jack dwelt on this morning, romance was becoming more of a mystery. The areas of what was known about each other, what could honestly be delivered, were reaching their edges as well. This was a gamble. Either retreat back to the open but limited glade of predictability, or venture into what was surely darkness fraught with revelation. The true and the false. That's what awaited them.

Wasn't it said at a men's gathering about a year ago that relationships with women are, for men, like going into "hostile enemy territory." Men don't know what is going on. They are relationship idiots, or should be considered as such because relationships are so alien to them; whereas women have an ease at its complexity. Well, that is almost obvious; but for women, being with a man must be like being with an alien. From Jack's experience, men went to the edge more often and many went gladly into the darkness. He didn't think this made relationships hostile. Hostile was a poor description. Intense, intimate, and unknown was more like it.

Jack walked into the bedroom with two coffees, And placed Gabriella's on the table, an old cigar stand by her side of the bed. He sat on the edge of the bed and took a sip. He crawled back to bed and watched Gabriella slowly waken. Her soft brown hair against a deep yellow pillow, the gentle bliss of nowhere lingers long. Irresistible.

"Good Morning, Honey," he paused to see if she was awake and listening. "I'm sitting here with my coffee and I was thinking for a moment, ..." he said cheerfully.

Gabriella opened her eyes, blinked, and smiled slowly. She took a sip of her coffee, winked, and settled in. Jack rubbed her shoulders and continued, "I was thinking about how easy it is to demand from life that life be perfect. Perfectly comforting with no surprises. Like, for instance, that my coffee be perfect. Not too cold, not too hot. But, who really sees this as a demand?"

Gabriella stared at Jack and frowned, "Jack, you are the only one I know who gets up first thing in the morning and wonders whether he is being too demanding of his coffee. Easy cowboy, give me a moment."

"I don't know, it's just a thought." Jack slid closer, kissed her on the cheek, "I can't help but notice that my life usually occurs as something I know, when it could just as easily occur as a mystery. Like you and me. I know about us, and I notice I want it to be a certain way. But, if I look truthfully, that want is really a demand, a demand that life be comfortable and predictable."

"Yeah. We all want that."

He looked at her cautiously, "Yes, we all do, I suspect, on some level. It's safe. And yet, don't we know it's not enough? Is it hard to see that a demand is not a simple preference, it's an absolute certainty of what is right? Our demands may exclude what is actually there or what is actually happening. They block what, I believe, is an ability to accept life as it occurs. To enjoy its perfect occurrence. Plus, a demand has so much wanting in it. But, does it bring us what we need?

"OK, I think I'm beginning to hear you. "I'll have another sip of coffee." Gabriella held her hands around the cup and pulled it slowly to her lips. "OK, Jack. I think I can listen now." She took another sip. "You're saying that we should accept that we demand rather than request things. We are demanding creatures that hide our demands, but pretend they are requests. In that way, we are covert about everything and deny it, or worse don't know it. Therefore, we have no choice about life. It's all habitual demands, all wanting without getting, perpetually upset that our demands are not met, without really noticing what we need, right?" She paused and quickly added, "And, that by seeing our demands for what they are, we might have a choice. A choice to go past wanting and actually get what we need."

Jack nodded his head in agreement, "Yes, that's right. Usually we have no choice because we don't notice how we are acting on our demands.

But we could notice this, get that it is an act, invented, and that we have a choice. A choice to be demanding or to be considerate of our ability to enjoy, explore, and witness what happens; and address our true needs. That is, we can have a choice either to demand from the Universe, often very specific things we want; or to be in service to its mysteries, which is something we need and are in fact designed to do."

Gabriella sighed, "Whew, didn't know if I would pass that exam." She smiled, "So, tell me, what are your needs?"

She slid closer to Jack, looked into his eyes, and said softly, "That has me think about us. When I think about us, that we are beginning to get closer and more intimate, and we only know so much about each other. When I think about that, I see that what you are saying is we won't go deeper and more intimate unless we accept our demands for what they are. Then maybe we can go on. Are you saying that maybe it is time to be less demanding and more adventurous?"

Jack smiled, "Yes, I think so. You've probably got it right. I think I'm asking, what are our demands, what are our needs? What are yours, what are mine?"

Gabriella rolled even closer and hooked her ankle around Jack's calf, "I'll think about it. Not that I have any problems with your demands."

A WHITTLED BRANCH OF LUM

—◁◁◁◁∩∭▷▷—

Reissa reached into his jeans, scouted a pink business card with turquoise blue lettering, *Molly Turbane – Hairdresser – By Appointment Only.* Whittled on the back in purple ballpoint ink were the words, "call me."

Molly's phone rang. Faux suspense, smiles, smirks, and lips tingled. "Dinner at 6?" Each anticipation, a promotion. Though they lurked, no promises yet. They waited, like puddles after a rain.

—◁◁◁◁∩∭▷▷—

Say "Yes"
bathe deep
each new demand
found quick

found by chance
chance found
What is obvious
is often found by chance

THE STUFF OF THE KOSMOS

The next day, Jack was up at 7am to take his car to the garage for inspection repairs. Shower, coffee, a toasted crunchy buttered bagel, the still quiet city streets; the early sun made shadows ballet, the apartment's stage walls softlit, while Gabriella slept.

Returning from the garage, Jack sat at his computer, "I have about one hour before Gabriella wakes up. This is good. A little private time to write and get ready. This is bliss sort of ... being alone. I admit it. Bliss in the real world. An acceptance of this life. It's sort of, as it is not always totally noticeable to me, but these past few mornings it has been. Seems that after almost two, no three months, I understand my life a bit more. It fits me better, or so it seems. My life keeps expanding, re-arranging, damming and demolishing, rebuilt and filling up again."

Checking his emails, Jack held his warm coffee, sipped it, and placed it on a note pad on his desk, where a ring formed halfway under the cup. The morning light was gray with simple hints of summer light and green. Gabriella woke up, got some coffee, and returned to bed. He wrote slowly.

"I have for a long time looked at what 'fulfillment' is, and I do this again this morning. This is what I have found: It's not just that I can be filled by life, but full of life as well in an ever-expanding existence. I see that fulfillment is dynamic – *it moves, it expands, it must be managed.* I would say there is a correlation between fulfillment and being open to life. Both expand and make room for existence to occur, which highlights a purpose, a mystery of life. That life is consciousness and consciousness is dynamic." He closed his eyes and the deeper male voice was felt. It began to guide his thoughts.

Jack called Gabriella.

She sat with him, arranged her recorder, and he nodded. She asked the guides, "Are you there? Are you ready to speak?"

Jacks began to speak in a deeper smoother voice.

"Life fulfills and expands with the witnessing of its existence. Consciousness is about being 'witness' to existence occurring. With no consciousness – witnessing existence is not dynamic. That is, it does not live or die, or struggle or communicate. It disappears as quickly as it occurs, without a laugh, without a whimper, or the appreciation of these things."

Jack paused.

Gabriella asked, "What do you mean by 'It disappears?'"

Jack swallowed, and continued.

"It is the witnessing, the noticing of physical, emotional, and contemplative occurrences as phenomena of the senses that create the opening for existence to express Itself. When we notice that we have the Kosmos's greatest gift: awareness, we see that this is the very stuff of life and the existence of the living mind. Awareness is the firmament of logos and the kinesthesia, the subtle energy, and the ethos of source. Awareness allows thought, which in its purist form is a dialogue between the witness and that which is witnessed. Awareness at its apex is the perception of the in-between. Without perception, there is nothing to be aware of, and no thought is available to express beauty. Perception brings the 'something' of existence to consciousness and is the essential partnership of existence and awareness. This marriage causes occurrence to transfer into action. It causes existence to bip and bop and boil. It causes what is to move.

"Is-ing, the movement of Being, occurs because awareness allows for a witnessing, a 'noticing' of existence. Existence is No-thing; the noticing of which causes Something to occur. 'Awakening' refers to being conscious, refers to the act of 'noticing' existence occurring. Usually we don't. Left on our own, we do

things automatically, in a sleep, and only, at best, sense parts of a dream. We virtually notice nothing let alone why something occurs. We may notice 'things,' but we almost always do not notice our 'noticing' of things. And this 'noticing our noticing' is a very unique potential, the potential of the witness. Without this, it, existence is unnoticed and remains Nothing. Witnessing isn't something mankind does without practice, even though it is who we are behind our thoughts, before we speak. It is a direct-observance of existence, of the truth, as it occurs. In this observation, there is a communion. Noticing takes practice. In this communion is a profound recognition. Recognition takes practice. Thou art that. And thou art that. And, thou art that.

"Communication is essentially the joy of recognition by reflection. The recognition of ourselves in the Other. This is what 'knowing' is. We only know the Other by getting more of ourselves. When we notice this and then speak, we transform Nothing into Something in each moment. On a noetic level, we are the witness of existence and the parents of our reality. 'Thou art that.' Awareness is the job of human potential. Making Nothing into Something. An enjoyable job."

Jack stopped speaking. He turned and stared out the window for a moment. Outside there were construction workers drilling and banging, the noise pressing through the thick cement walls. He noticed the world waking up and starting to build things. Looking at his computer, he noticed he received an email from Susanna.

Gabriella stood and put a hand on Jack's shoulder. She leaned over and said to him, "I got it." Tucking her recorder in her hand, she walked into the living room.

PARIS IS A BORE

Dearest Jack:

Paris is a bore. Oh no, it isn't. It can't be. No.

Tell me, Jack-o'-lantern of mine, are we "out there?" Because sometimes I'm not sure if I'm anywhere, really accomplishing anything.

Are we, am I, on a voyage, mission, an exploration? Sent by whomever? And if so, why was I chosen for this mission? Why did I volunteer? Why didn't I prepare better? Personally, I didn't think it would be so difficult. Or, do we toil like Sisyphus continuing to do the same over and over again never getting anywhere. Is there anything else to do?

Last night, as I was lying in bed watching TV, I thought that if you really wanted to live on the edge of civilization's accomplishments, the best job would be engineering, space engineering. Building those space shuttles and satellites, and seeing what would happen. That is advanced work. Plus you would get a keen view of the rest of the planet.

Now, at this moment I wonder, why do I think these things? Am I saying I want a high-end job? Does being at the high end drive me? Looking down from on high? Does that give me my kicks, my yah yahs? The answer to that is yes. I think it does, but I can't say my elation/bliss meter went higher with that yes. No, definitely it didn't; nor did I expect it to. Because it may just be the same old thing all over again just in new wrapping.

What I expect is revelation. Genuine epiphany, a realization of godliness. No, even more. Direct God-In-My-Face, but I'm not sure I would recognize it if I actually saw it. So, my expectation is unformed. Like my mission, I suppose. Incomplete, which adds up to a mortifying conclusion: I'm just treading water. This is why I feel this way. This is why I feel annoyed. My research has been so-so. I guess.

I'm almost finished and will be coming back to New York soon.

Love, Susanna

⟞⟝

Susanna:

Writing back just to connect. Sitting here after a long schvitz at the Russian Baths. It's nice to go back there now and then. The last time I was there was with you and Reissa last fall. I'm a bit fatigued, uneasy. No, just fatigued; having made significant accomplishments in the past week. Nonetheless, feeling worn out, and yet, also odd glimpses of being settled.

<"Are we, am I, on a voyage, mission, an exploration?">

When I read that, I heard this from my guides, "*Life is unfolding in a unique harmony and the challenge is to step up to a higher level of communication*". You might want to consider that.

I see that as what is waiting to unfold for all of us.

<Is there anything else to do?>

Yes, we can be on purpose; we can share our thoughts, feelings, and imaginations; we can ask for help. We can see others as ourselves; unlike Sisyphus, we can stop if we choose not to accept that consequence; we can just leave the boulder at the bottom of the hill.

Lately, with the help of Gabriella, I have been looking into "healing" and healing ministry. There's no specific ideology except that I'd become accountable as a healer in the specific way I heal, and to be clear about my direct contact with "source" as the source of my ability to heal. I'm starting to see in my consulting work that what I do is heal communities, whether they're corporations, neighborhoods, or shopping centers. Others heal bodies or emotions or spirit. There is something about accepting our ability to heal and to be "At-Source" that is the key to surrendering to a purpose that transcends the Sisyphus condition of perpetually shuffling life's karmic boulders.

What I'm getting from this is that you too can choose to have a "ministry" that is what you are accountable for, a joyful useful service. You can choose to be honest about that and not hide from it. Acknowledging our ministry, our inner light, and our healing gift in some small way, gives our lives joy at any time; and in a huge way has us able to push much more substantial boulders. We get to push the whole context of consciousness to greater and greater holons. That's what Arthur Koestler called them, holons. Holons are phenomena that are whole unto themselves and also comprised of parts, which are just smaller wholes, and at the same time a part of a greater whole, a context, which is part of lesser and lesser and greater and greater context – all at the same time.

Awareness, that is noticing, begins with being aware of the context we are in; the whole that we are part of. Transformation is creating and being aware of the context that your context is in. Context-Holons, within context-holons, all the way up and down the ladder of existence from the smallest infinity to the largest infinity, never ending. We move life itself along through this matrix. The boulder that rolls back down is not the same stone we retrieve and assist in its ascent. It has transformed, evolved. After 1000 times pushing, slipping, retrieving, maybe we get that this is what humanity does. And, we transcend.

Yet, life still looks like life. That is, we don't notice everything or anything all the time. Our feelings about life go up and down. But, a healer has a sense of direction: service; and lives more in the "what" of life, the context, rather than the "how," the content.

See you when you return.

All my Love,
Jack O'Lantern-lit

WHAT IS NEVER LOST

For three solid days there was an odd continuation of morning fog lasting all day. Morning didn't seem to cease until about an hour before sundown.

At sundown, Reissa and Molly met at the corner of Mott and Canal Street, turned north up Mott and headed into the Oriental Pearl for dinner. Chance encounters that turn into years together and last deep into the night have no mercy, no reprieve.

Molly's short tight black skirt bounced laughingly, and Reissa's light pink shirt over khaki pants illuminated him as they left the restaurant full of moo shu shrimp. He gently held her waist and felt her hip tense and then tease. As they walked, their hair bounced in unison and mingled when the evening breeze picked up. Steam misted from the open markets. Chinese broccoli heaped high swam beside dry salted fish. Snails, slugs, and turtles in shallow plastic basins squirmed and yammered with very little hope to meet the right girl or guy.

East 6th Street seemed less crowded than it used to be. A musty view of dreams that happened twenty years ago – gone, yet lingering. The anxious dye of tainted and hopeful gatherings over chicken vindaloo and naan. Here men gather to meet the new young waitress. A small pippish gal with wide eyes and curves, cute, so girly cute and known. Sweet and full of greet, mango chutney sweet, sweet enough for everyone and more. This faded, but not before the evening ended and she showed it all and gave it all away for trinkets.

Gabriella and Jack walked down East 6th Street and across First Avenue, and headed into The Caravan of Dreams, a cozy basement vegetarian restaurant. They ordered curried vegetable stew and sipped organic wine in the comfy den. Gabriella leaned back in the wooden pew against the wall to listen to Jack play piano at the far end of the room, singing in his smoky voice. The chef stopped cooking, nodding his head to Jack's funky blues and crunchy growl, "Sittin' at the corner of a crowded saloon. Flippin' a quarter-like gold doubloon. Now, didn't I, didn't I, catch your eye?"

Susanna boarded a plane in Paris for JFK Airport and sat down next to what turned out to be Frank Sinatra's nephew, dressed in a dark blue corporate business suit and red tie. They smiled and chatted. The plane went high, then suspended, night crowds speak softly and huddle in hiss and hum. Later Susanna whispered, "follow me," and toward the back they went. Restroom cramped and immediate. Eyes wide open must be deep, deeply unexpected. She swallowed as the plane glided smooth. Susanna rose with a gulp.

The Manhattan night hung in warm spring air. Leaves were blooming full again, but had not given up their fight. Not yet. On a park bench by the river there was a frivolous moan. A twinkle of pink lit up a smile buried deep in tan.

At midnight, Jack lay sleeping naked against Gabriella. The bow of her back shoulders an angel's silent wish. A wish of curve and beauty forged from leap, tan and supple taunt, cupped man about woman. His lips against a living neck, frivolous light and sneaky wisps of elflike hair and human warm breath. Here, then gone. Held in heat, his leg slid and ankles touched in what is never lost.

A MURMUR OF REGRET

—⊶⊷—

Susanna waved goodbye and walked down the airport corridor to the taxis.

Into the midnight
of our last kiss
Is it really our last kiss?

—⊶⊷—

Dawdle, cawed, mute and gendered
bobby kiss and lee
St. Lum wiggle.

St. Lum and wiggle
bent in the night
sit together on a plane
binky head on Bobby
settled sense of sonar gone good
one tone leads to another
one breath leads to embrace

Heard and willed
a murmur of regret
that life organic comes and goes

... it does ...
and with it mystery

Reach across and
feel that life is within your grasp
without
a cry a rage a wager gone badly
pitting sorrow against any jove
or any witty reflection
that in the tenderest whispers
would die for lack of air
we shall not
forget a child's tender steps

it is without warning that we crumble
without warning
we cave
into whimper and doubt
there is no memory of what we held last night
only a bitter tang in angled mist and pot
and that held in horror
lonely and molting into the midnight of our last kiss

unless of course
we watch our words
with care
and notice where they come from

LISTEN – GOD IS SPEAKING

Jack and Gabriella waken. It's 4am. The city is quiet and polite. A gentle alto voice nudges in, *"Wake up."* A familiar dream voice, lush and sensuous with nixal heat. Apiaceous, delicious, and pimping with pike. Pancake warm with wrap and houma, tame and welcome. Jack got up and dressed in his favorite dark gray cotton sweater, blue jeans, and old leather moccasins. Gabriella dressed in her favorite jeans and oversized red cotton sweater; she pulled on her overcoat and a lightweight scarf. He put on a light coat and red baseball cap; then walked up to the roof to grab two plastic lawn chairs in the stairwell before stepping outside. He put the chairs down near the western edge of the roof and remained standing, facing west with the river backlit. Gabriella settled down with pen and paper and a digital recorder. A hint of dawn is urgent as if a secret is about to be revealed. Jack sat and nodded towards Gabriella, who smiled excitedly.

Gabriella sat up, leaned forward and said, "I am listening." A moment passed, the Westside highway hummed softly in the foreground, a cool breeze blew up from the river through the canyons and towards the east behind him. Manhattan was remarkably quiet, anticipating. Jack spoke in a gentle lilting alto voice.

"You may have heard us say before, 'to listen as if God is speaking.' Listening to the world this way is the access to Authenticity, to Truth.

"It is false of mankind not to listen in this way. It is not true to man's nature. But, most can hardly be with this kind of listening. It is felt as too intimate, too bold. Or, that in some way it diminishes the listener. This is the cause of all suffering.

"When we listen this way, what it is, what is heard, is a message. An invitation to the miraculous. We say this because the desire to listen in this way is often obscured, almost forgotten and lost. More accurately, it is misplaced and replaced with false ideas. And, because of this, mankind is unprepared to acknowledge its most powerful potential. The power of creation, of being creative."

Jack paused and seemed to shuffle in his chair. He started to speak again, but the voice had changed to a medium range male voice, just as gentle and at ease.

"Look and see how unprepared mankind is to 'greet' Authenticity; to listen as if God is speaking. If you watch carefully, it is still difficult for people to accept

the idea of this 'Authentic Reality' as being immediately available to them. This is not because people are unable – far from it. It is because of the conditions around the way people are taught to listen. These conditions are part of the current language of inauthenticity, which has man focus on the individual as more important than the community. This focus does not allow us to listen to Authentic Reality effectively, or at all. It has us misunderstand this way of listening and thwarts the advance of a new language.

"We may think that if we are talking about something other than ourselves or another person, that we are listening to Authentic Reality. That is not true. To do this correctly, we have to listen to ourselves and others in the context of a community dialogue rather than as competing monologues. This is accomplished by considering that when a person talks, it is not them talking; it is the community, like God, choosing to speak through that particular person. It is also accomplished by not only going beyond planning the next thing to say, and not only listening for where the conversation is going, but listening for the reality that is being created in each moment, in each emerging conversation." Here, Jack paused.

Gabriella spoke, "I hear you. May I ask a question?"

Jack nodded affirmatively.

"Are you saying I am not speaking?" inquired Gabriella.

Jack replied, but this time the deeper male voice spoke.

"You are speaking, but you are not separate from the source of your speaking. Listen as if everything said to you is there to empower you. Your listening is the womb of existence. Let what is said grow and develop in your listening."

"I don't think I'm that powerful," Gabriella said matter-of-factly, shifting in her chair. She stared across the rooftops.

She heard Jack say, *"But, you are. Pay attention. You are creating your reality. That thought just came into reality. Not wrong or right, just so. But, is that what you need? Is that your truth? I would ask you, who just said that? Was it you? Or, did it come from an old place, an inheritance? Maybe you have something else to say."*

Gabriella, "I don't know." She watched the breeze blow Jack's jacket a bit. A pair of pigeons perked their heads, spread their wings, and quickly lifted off the adjacent roof heading north up the river valley.

"Listening only as an individual gives us a world of conditions, judgments, beliefs, and associations that separate us from each other. Our interest and love are conditional within a framework of insistent individuality. The most crippling condition is a

prevalent theory that the Universe is not 'big enough' for the unveiling of each and every voice. Man lives in a resignation that tells us we do not belong and will not be heard, that we are not capable of accomplishing very much. And so, we hide; we are not present and our full voice is never heard. It is this new voice of community, the Authentic Reality of a new context of Being, that fulfills us; this is what we wish to share with you this morning. We will show you a way to step past your conditions, and to unconditionally maximize human potential.

"Unconditionality occurs when we face the unknown and surrender what we know of ourselves to what we will never know. But rarely is this surrender complete. **It is the will to surrender that causes awakening.** *Therefore, once awakened, much of what is surrendered is returned, often upgraded. That which is not returned is a small price to pay, a token.*

Jack stopped, stood up, and stretched. He walked around the rooftop and sat back down.

Gabriella looked straight at him; their eyes connected and she said reassuringly, "It's going well."

Jack smiled and said, "I know." They both smiled and kissed. Jack took a breath and the alto voice spoke.

"There is a false theory employed by mankind that causes humanity to be conditional. It is linked to the Quantum

Theory of Love. It is another background conversation, taken for granted and accepted unwittingly as truth. It is the cause of much suffering. This theory says that the Universe is not big enough, as I stated earlier, for the acknowledgement of each and every voice. This is not true. Its message has become a deep cultural hypnosis of poverty. As participants, people are marionettes in a sleeping state. It is the crux of a paradox occurring in your perception at the intersection of all that is limited by all that is unlimited. What you see in this theory is only one side of things, or one possibility. The theory is based on a false understanding of perception that says, because you have a limited perspective, it must also mean everything else is limited. The theory disappears when you see that each perspective is an aspect sourced from unlimited possibilities, and each perspective is a reflection as well as a portal to the unlimited."

A moment passed. Gabriella and Jack waited. Jack began to speak again; the voice was more medium-toned – not deep, not light – a mellow tenor.

"To get the paradox and free ourselves of the false theory, we must take an absolute stand to listen as if God is speaking to us. We must be committed to understanding the paradox and to exposing the truth that the Universe is abundant, regardless of ideas to the contrary. To understand this, we must experience it; and that takes great courage.

"Most importantly, we must be accountable for our commitment to this quest. That is, be someone who

can be counted on to be 100% committed to this listening. This accountability is Wisdom's charge. True commitment generates complete intention; any less will result in failure.

"Nothing new can occur, no new ground can be broken unless you are 100% committed. 90% committed would leave 10%, and that 10% would be 100% non-committed. Being less than 100% is the basis of our delusions." Jack stopped speaking.

Gabriella took the opportunity to say, "I don't know if I am 100% committed to everything or even some things. How can I be 100% committed?"

Jack spoke again in the deeper voice.

"In truth, there is no such thing as a commitment being less than 100%. Less than 100% is wishing. Without commitment, we cannot expect much. 100% is what true commitment is, because only then can we honestly say we have courage. If we are less than 100% committed we are not able to greet Authenticity, since this requires the surrender of all we know. And this requires true courage, the courage to not-know, trust and to create. We can tell we are not fully committed when we rely only on what we know, and dwell in feelings, judgments, and familiarity. This indicates that we are not prepared to act courageously.

"To wake up and greet Authenticity honorably requires 100% commitment. Remember, commitment is not

knowledge or what we know. We must stand completely in what is possible, on the edge of droxis, which is all that is known and spoken. Standing at this edge, we can leap into the Unknown. Either we leap or we don't. We cannot partly leap. If we're caught between courage and comfort, we will surely stumble. This leap requires 100%; anything less than 100% is no leap, no advance, no awakening. It's easy. Touch your heart, then leap. Your heart will beat strongly. You will know it's there, without a doubt. You will be alive. (There is a short pause) Remember, everything we tell you is about being alive. Live!"

The voice ended and a cool breeze blew across the roof, rustling a scrap of paper in a corner of the roof's walls, the sounds echoing within the three-foot rise above the roof. The sun backlit the east in dark red and orange. Jack sat down and asked, "If I am committed to this path, how do I know it is 'God' who is speaking?"

NOT-I

The sky was still dark, but a full light began to emerge on the eastern horizon. The shamanic male voice began speaking to Jack and Jack saw Truman in his thoughts. He told Gabriella this.

Gabriella went downstairs and returned with a large glass of water. Jack drank. "It's almost daytime", she said to him. He laughed, "Let's go on a bit more. I don't think they're finished yet. A chatty bunch, eh?"

Gabriella sat down and waited, then spoke to Jack, "Is there anything else?"

He nodded and the deep male voice spoke.

"We know when God is speaking by distinguishing 'Not-I' from 'I.' Therefore, once we understand commitment, we must then distinguish Not-I. This begins the path of Truth, to Authentic Reality, to the Divine. I will now speak of Not-I and our humanity, which is based on it The path of truth begins here.

"Not-I is a partial reality."

Gabriella broke in and asked, "Why?" The voice answered.

"Our personal ego, or the concept of 'me' or 'mine,' is Not-I – as are all known senses of identity. Not-I is what we call ourselves, and our sense of the world. Not-I separates us from other things. When we say, 'I am not this, and I am not that,' we are experiencing Not-I. Authentic Reality, the Divine singularity, is much more than this. It is 'I', whole and complete; all that is, and all that is not. It is the transcendent identity. 'I' integrates you with all things. One thing/ All things. Courage is the willingness to surrender the Not-I to the Authentic-I, to what we essentially are, a peace that passes all understanding. This is the path of truth, our truth. The path of truth is a path of peace, the path of surrendering our limitations to our greatness.

"The Authentic "I" and "We" are one, not unlike a drop of rainwater that falls into the ocean. It is a whole unto itself, but it is a part of a greater whole.

"At every level of being, we are whole and also a part of a greater whole – from the smallest to the greatest, all the way up and all the way down the infinite ladder of existence. We are whole and a part of a greater whole. One glimpse, one look, one listen, one whiff is all we need to be At-Source."

There was a moment of silence and Gabriella looked up at Jack, who sat looking ahead. She said, "Tell me more about being At-Source."

The deeper voice returned.

"One of the first discoveries on the path of truth is that there is no againstness. Againstness is not understanding the whole that we are, or resisting the whole we are becoming. That way of thinking is a contracting rather than expanding force. We can proceed when we understand that the "not" in Not-I, is not a negation but an affirmation of the unknowing, unknowable source of all existence. Not-I is a process of knowing by transforming what is not-known into what is known. At-Source, mankind is whole and complete. We all experience it, in each moment, as partnership; each part and the whole partnership as one Reality. The knowing of everything in each moment is joyously unavailable. But, humanity can reflect on its possibilities; reveal, use, and experience its presence in the hierarchy of partnerships at every level of being, all the way up and all the way down the expanding Kosmos."

The alto voice returned, faded in.

"We can be thankful for Not-I, limitations, our illusions. They are not permanent; they only appear to be. Revealing them for what they are is the access to truth, potential, and power. This revelation allows us to honestly accept what we do not know, just as It is, a source of creation. Knowing that life is a work of art, a creation, is something we all can enjoy. Truth, for us, is always a reflection. It grows and develops continuously. As an unfolding reflection of Reality,

life remains an exploration, a mystery awakened by the language that defines it. The good news is, we are the language inventors. All we obtain is a reflection of ourselves. Whatever we perceive, is Us, goodness."

REFLECTING THE AUTHENTIC

Dawn broke to a dark fire burnt against the horizon and the roof was in a hushed gray light. A bruise of blue sky solid and true appeared in swatches and streaks. The guide's voice trailed off as if to rest. A crisp clean breeze blew suddenly like a flame. The upper clouds were white with anticipation; the buildings below a dark cragged silhouette. The deeper male voice returned quietly at first, then it filled Jack's thoughts.

Jack spoke.

"When we are able to listen to what is authentic about others and ourselves, and examine what we discover, only then will we come to understand ourselves as a reflection of Authentic Reality. The idea that the reflection is everything is obviously an illusion. When we listen as if God is speaking, we listen to our reflection of what is the authentic Divine. We do this with a simple phrase, "Thank you." Gratitude is not an illusion, and we connect to Authentic Reality by being grateful. When we turn towards this Reality, we turn towards our true unlimited Self. We are At-Source. This is purposeful. The reality we create is derived from

Authentic Reality; it has it within it. This is why it is real, in the sense that it is created.

"Our reality is observable because it is pregnant with possibility. A simpler truth is: Reality births what is possible as an ever-occurring phenomenon. Moment to moment as a continuous invitation. This, however, is not how mankind usually sees life. We see the reflection of reality as an actuality that has permanence; but this permanence is sustained only in memory. Memory is not the full reflection, but a fragmented reflection that has a negotiated place and time. Suffering builds when memory fades, as it always does, being true to its nature. Suffering becomes sustained when memory is replaced by myth and make believe. Suffering occurs in the story we give it, and becomes traumatic in the demand that the story be true. To know mankind in this forgetful state is to know a creature snoring fitfully in a dream that never stays the same, demanding that the dream remains unchanged."

The eastern sky suddenly broke forth with streaming volcanic color. Jack and Gabriella sat in the lawn chairs and waited. A few airplanes in the distant sky, rising straight and true, winked with silver light.

NETI NETI

Jack got up and walked around the rooftop watching the sunrise, its bright light ripping across Manhattan. Gabriella joined him.

The female voice began to speak to them.

"Of course, a reflection isn't what it appears to be. It is an indirect reality, not a direct experience. The moment the reflection is said to be "It," as in "that's it, that's the truth, the ultimate reality;" we can be assured it is not, as we cannot truly perceive this. The reflection isn't the Truth.

"We must understand that we are not designed to live in a complete understanding of the Authentic. We are able to have the courage to create and go beyond fear, however; and surrender and turn towards Truth. To face with courage and accept straight on the unknowingness, the void, of Authenticity, and be thankful."

Gabriella asked, "Tell me more about the unknown."

The deeper voice spoke.

"Our truth is available when knowing is surrendered to what we don't know. This opportunity is available and occurs in each moment. Mankind invents what is by declaring what is possible and acting on that declaration. By surrendering to creation, we are recreated. In this way, failure brings mankind to success. We discover our true nature to invent language, which manages our reality; and speak our discoveries from an unlimited Source. Language conceptualizes consciousness and allows mankind to live as created beings. That's our job. Mankind is designed to embrace the reflection of Authenticity as an ongoing exploration, and structure its discoveries in language. Man invents language to structure experience and discoveries of the unknown as something known. This is the world we live in.

"It is time to walk to the edge of language, the edge of the known and spoken world, the edge of droxis. Face that unknown, and leap."

THE NEOLOGIST

Dawn fully emerged. Stoney silhouettes resolved into buildings with roof gardens and trees. Jack stretched and sat again, as the alto voice returned. He opened his eyes and looked at Gabriella who seemed wide awake. He listened and spoke from the deep voice.

"We refer to 'Reflecting the Authentic' as standing in endless unfolding possibilities. One mind. Speaking our truth. Accepting all that is and all that is not. No demands. Generating the eternal. Actualizing the moment by speaking it. A conscious source of reality, and speaking that reality into being.

"Mankind is invited by the Kosmos to invent language that expresses the possibilities of existence and to embrace the unfolding of Truth, Beauty, and Goodness. Mankind fulfills an ancient and exquisite promise to reflect the Authentic and express its discoveries in a living world. To thrive in this promise is to be a source of existence itself, of evolution, transformation, and power. To live fully is to grasp this promise and live it. When we have the courage to face the unknown and step beyond fear, language emerges as a fundamental tool

that is accountable for new worlds; for new reflections of the Authentic."

Here the voice changed to the tenor.

"Our language is a network of the conversations mankind creates and exists in. It is this network of conversations that is life, the known reality, for mankind. The community maintains this network as the common voice, and all conversations in the network belong to the community. New conversations sourced from the unknown have existence in reality when they become part of the community.

"To be accountable for evolution is to be the source for new conversations in the community. To be this source is to be transformational. What is possible are completely new conversations, new aspects of language and communication that bring new ways of being into our reality. Those who live At-Source and invent new conversations are the leaders of their communities, accountable for its successes and able to transform each individual voice into the voice of the community."

Again there was a moment of silence; the sun had completely risen and was shining brightly. The deeper voice spoke.

"When someone is "At-Source," they have turned towards Authentic Reality, the Divine, the source of all things possible. They reflect and embrace the gifts of the experience. In great compassion and gentleness,

they turn and are renewed. As they speak, they speak not only for themselves, but disappear as an individual and become aware of being the "community of consciousness" that turns as they turn. In this way, the Kosmos is reversed and mankind parents divinity into everyday living existence with the divine as child and the community of mankind its parent. Wonderfully playful, the Divine responds with a beginners mind, and mankind has the potential to speak as an elder.

"The language mankind invents reflects and expresses the Divine – Authentic Reality, and exists as mankind's common voice. Community is the full expression of humanity's consciousness at any moment and time. It is where reality manifests Itself as a creative act, as art. Who we are is a network of conversations. Forever changing, forever describing, forever transforming the community that we are."

A warm breeze blew across the roof from the west. Sounds of morning traffic still seemed careful not to disturb the quiet. The Jersey cliffs of the Hudson River palisades shimmered brightly in morning light and were reflected on the water below.

THE LANGUAGE OF LISTENING

Jack pulled his arms in and held himself close. The sun suddenly peeked fully above a cloud on the horizon, sending a ray of light across the city. A peregrine falcon glided slowly above the buildings. Jack smiled and pointed this out to Gabriella, raising his chin and speaking out loud to the falcon and the soft blaze reflecting off the Hudson River, "It is a pleasure seeing you again." He was answered by the deep male voice; Gabriella again recorded him.

"This prepares us to leap off the edge of language and listen to Authentic Reality. What will initially show up are our limitations.

"Listen deeper. Notice that initially, you do not listen to others, the in-between, or from what is possible. We listen mostly to the same familiar, persistent inner voices. Acknowledge this and notice the small world these voices live in. Notice how familiar it is and let those conversations drift into the background.

"Listen deeper. Surrender. Let Authenticity emerge in your complete listening. Look at this listening. Let it be

complete with full body, mind, and spirit existing in the space between ourselves and another. Our whole being awake in dialogue. All that is emerges with ease as a clear path of discovery in each moment. We are sourced directly, intimately, and completely from the Authentic Divine Reality continuously. In each moment, we are witnessed into an existing reality, birthed by awareness, and caressed by consciousness; awareness is awakened and cared for by the language of the Universe.

"Listen deeper. All we seek exists as what we say it is. All occurs, now, always, in each moment. Parented by language, we invent what exists in our reality. We hold the moment in beauty. Truth is reflected in the basic goodness of life, shared by language and its lullabies.

"Listen deeper. Everything said and done empowers us. We are here to empower each other."

Jack got up and walked around the rooftop, near the edge, seventeen floors up, and looked west across the buildings. He noticed the reflection of full morning light on Manhattan. Gabriella wrote a few notes, turned off the recorder, and stood up. "Jack, let's go downstairs for a moment. I need some coffee."

GRATITUDE

On the edge of droxis
Awaken
And leap
To speak a new reality
Where one becomes
Community
Where who I am
becomes
a partnership

Thank you

They came back up to the roof about fifteen minutes later, coffee in hand. The voices in Jack's thoughts paused, as if in contemplation. Present, silent, watchful. The slow ease of early car traffic far below seems barely audible, somewhat lazy. Meandering with only a slight adhesion to the morning quiet. You can almost hear folks stretch before getting out of bed to wash and brush and shower on their way to a new day. As though a friend put a careful arm across Jack's back, the female voice returned and spoke invitingly. Jack knew the guides were there..

"We are listening."

Jack turned to Gabriella and said to her, "I believe we have a bit more to go." Gabriella found her notepad and pen, and turned on the recorder.

She said, "We're here. Please speak. Tell me about power."

The voice continued.

"Awakening to community as One's self reveals consciousness. The foundation of community is partnerships. The willingness to empower others and be empowered. Effective in its fullness and completion, in its impact and versatility, in its curiosity and ability to grow. That is, we can observe the unconsciousness of 'me-ism' versus the opportunity of "we-consciousness' emerging."

The female voice departed and the deeper male voice began speaking to Gabriella slowly and deliberately.

"The opportunity available for mankind is to expand the understanding of dignity. Value each individual as a source of creation and a full expression of the community. Without dignity, there is no access to humanity. Giving dignity to the world-as-community

is what awaits mankind. In a world where dignity is not divine, man's inhumanity to man will have no bounds.

"Dignity is found not only by what is done, made, or accomplished; but by what is found to be good in its simplest form. And, to express gratitude. This simple and fundamental good provides access to being aware of the greatness of life, and to connect all that is good to that which has it be so. Dignity is easier to access than previously thought. It is available the moment someone notices what is good in each moment and in each occurrence. Recognizing the good awakens consciousness and becomes a light of truth. In this way, dignity is a practice of being aware of basic goodness. We do this by expressing gratitude."

The tenor voice returned.

"There is dignity in recognizing individuality. There is wonderful dignity in recognizing that each person is not simply a fated cog in a chaotic Kosmic plan; but a unique expression of life in pursuit of beauty, goodness, and truth, with each soul equally possessing divinity. To leave it at that, however, and not recognize or respect the community voice, the great communal presence behind each utterance, uplifting not just the one, but the whole in each uplifted voice – causes all suffering.

The voices departed and Jack stood with Gabriella for a while on the roof. Time slowed down. Eventually, they picked up the chairs and put them away before going downstairs. In Jack's apartment, they took off their shoes. Jack washed his hands in the kitchen sink and made more coffee. He kissed Gabriella gently. They stood facing, holding hands saying nothing for a few moments. Both with smiles. Gabriella broke the embrace and got dressed. Before she left for work, she came up behind Jack who was already sitting at his computer, leans over and with a soft hug she kisses him on the cheek. "Thank you," She lingers a bit and then leaves.

YOU CAN COUNT ON ME

Accountability
rests
silently in a cradle
of vibration
songs spun to the listening
an embrace held deeper and tighter
than the pattern of hand
like the bread
of a curved and gentle sigh
it is the clay of our tomorrow

each vibration invites a longing for its essence
birthed anew at personal twilight
the in-between within and without
an unexpressed smile, intimate hugs
of collective unseen whispering
of what shall now unfold
in the disappearance of our mutual boundaries
into the future
we generate us

into the future we generate
we generate and captivate
a vaporous hush

in the taste of
anticipation

a pause

in wink and tart taste lip
and kiss
humbled and waiting
in wakeful first hello

and in the break of our departing
did we notice our sensibilities
fought in holds that shallowed our every look?

did I hear you say
you found me
with an echo?

and left with comet breath and ease
and left your crumbs for me to follow

—◦◦◦◦◦◦◦—

Jack sat at his computer finishing the poem and emailed it to Gabriella. Writing out a report for one of his clients, his work day began; he labored until just before sundown.

—◦◦◦◦◦◦◦—

Later that evening, Truman called.

"What up chuck?" Jack grunted. "Where are you?"

"I'm still in Maine, at home. Been out walking a bit." He paused. "I understand you've been hearing voices, old man," Truman said with a chuckle.

"Yes, I did. I mean, I am. It's amazing. Last night it lasted almost the entire night until sunrise. I heard them and spoke their words aloud. Gabriella recorded the whole thing. How did you know?"

"So Jack, you're a 'channeler' now. Well, what can I say? I was out taking a morning walk along the beach this morning right at dawn and came to the place we sat at by the river. It was about 6am. A falcon came across the horizon and sat on that very same tree, and I knew it had come that day to visit us. That's a good sign, but it also took me back to that day."

"I don't know, Truman; there's a lot of information. It just happened. It's been happening. You started it."

"What are you going to do?" Truman asked.

"I think I'm going to take it seriously. Gabriella is amazing; she has a real skill with it. They seem to speak to her. Maybe we'll share it. But, I'm also a little more sure of what I'm doing and what I want to teach. Yes, teach rather than just consult." Jack paused, "Thank you."

"Yes, I got that too. Your time has come. It also may be time to move. I hear Colorado and Montana are very nice. Maybe you should set up a place where people come to you. That's what I get." He paused, "Gotta go. We'll talk again."

"Truman, it's about partnerships. That's what I'm getting ... Truman. Truman, you there?" Truman had already hung up the telephone. Jack looked at the phone, shook his head. "Montana."

244

GOD'S GREAT NOODLE

—◁◁◁◁◁ᗡ〇ᗡ▷▷▷▷▷—

Existence comes from Nothing and becomes
Something when we say so.

Sitting for breakfast, bowl of gruel and cup o' joe
Writing recommendations
Twiddilin' expectations
Nudgin' God's great noodle ... the brain
The little medulla that could

It's been two days since the guides spoke to him.
Jack sometimes heard the shamanic male guide and
his own thoughts recite poems simultaneously.
He stared out the window and thought, "I kept
hearing the words 'on the edge of droxis.' And now
I see what it means. It means standing on the edge
of consciousness, the edge of all that is conscious
to mankind. When you are at the edge, you've
made it out of the safety zone, all clichés. You've
ventured past everyday conversations to the
edge of language. You stare out into the immense
silence of possibility, of all Being. Listening to all
the noise of humanity behind you, staring into the
silence ahead, what might you say now?" Then the
female voice spoke to him.

"That is what it is for us to know our truest nature. It is the inquiry we all may ask if we explore our true source. And, in so doing, come to an end of what has been said. Having toiled, slithered, bartered, and blithered past all that has been spoken to eventually arrive teetering on the very edge of the known Universe. Past the periphery and on the precipice. Having arrived at the beginning of the unknown Universe. This is the nothing that becomes something in the grace to make it so by speaking its name."

Jack could already hear the response to these thoughts. But this time, it was one of the male voices, the deep voice.

"The nothing that requests a voice. We've arrived here to yodel. To invent what there is to be said. We are on the edge of droxis. The noise behind dares to push us off the precipice. If we have our wits about us, we will leap, yodeling merrily, and we leap for everyone."

Jack wrote.

do our best swan dive
say what we have to say
yodeling rooster babble
tao flin und yipple batoom ba-tomb eir blain und feult
ratune
simmer lear from bitter nasturnum
battle the rull and ripple
sweet to touch and bathed in niff … and washed in
first water

with back in graceful arch
invent the conversations of life
from Nothing

SHIP OF HOPE

Molly sank slowly in a warm bath fit with lavender and spice. Reissa slipped in with her. Two bent angels bathed and two found fingers touched and bodies slipped in water warm, pretty, twined thighs and buttock bunch, pander in a puppy slither, rimmy rip and rummy wash. This brought a smile to Molly. Eyes closed, Reissa laid at peace, warm water up to his chin. He held Molly in a single vow.

Lip bittle
Spot of drip
Devours in a full wet birth

Steam lifts like mist across a thousand islands
Where wood and water peat
Where ship of hope meets dawn of temper
The timber of grace
The rain of remembrances

He washed her back with rose petals and smoothed the arc of her hip. He rubbed his head against her neck, his nose behind her ear. And there, the bend of body filled the bill the body knew as better water. That water filled the cup that every ocean mellows.

TWIXT BEAT AND BOB

The phone rang and Jack answered. It's Susanna, having returned from Paris to talk about her trip, the men she met, the tango lessons she took. Gabriella walked behind Jack, as he sat at his desk talking on the telephone. She was naked. As he talked, she gently bumped her breasts against his head and giggled.

Luscious brush and bait
continued
His face awash in twixt beat and bob,
restraint rocked in booby
A fact that fantasy can't match
It breaks the hold of any loneliness
The myth of time's tortured wait for just this moment,
just this thing deliciously applied and meandering to
what's next
Here, grief is forgotten
Forgotten for what once was
The doubt; if it could be again
Wondering if it ever was

"What did you do the day before you left?" Jack asked Susanna.

"A day with memories, good food and unique purchases, funny explorations and sightseeing. I bought some street art and a few garments. Different than most days, when I had little time for that sort of thing. Something shifted as I went back and forth," Susanna went on, "and my flight back was different. I met a guy, Bob, on the plane. Believe it or not, he was Frank Sinatra's nephew! We hit it off. I don't know. I think I acted a bit crazy. We had sex."

"Sex! Where?" Jack was stunned.

"Yes, on the plane. In the bathroom. It was daft, but fun."

"You're kidding? With a stranger?"

"Yes, I guess so," Susanna hesitated.

"When did you start having sex with strangers, Susanna?

"If you think about it, Jack, we always do that. We're always strangers at first, right?" She did her best Texas drawl on that last word.

"Yes, but, what are you talking about? What does that have to do with it? There is a huge step between lovers and strangers. Isn't there? Jesus!" said Jack.

"Evidently not. Cool down. That's my point. Sometimes that step moves in faster than at other times. It does happen you know."

Jack got more agitated, "It isn't that phantasmagorical Susanna and you know it. I mean, follow your heart, your interest, your attractions. But, there is being appropriate and responsible. Everything has a consequence. Getting away with a dire consequence doesn't make something appropriate. Does it?"

"Hey, I feel odd enough already. It felt good. What do you want from me? I shouldn't have said anything to you," Susanna spoke apologetically.

There is a moment of silence and Jack spoke a bit more carefully, "No, I am just concerned about you. You said you felt odd. That worries me. Why feel odd if you did what you wanted?"

Susanna paused, "It wasn't exactly the norm. It was risky and if it wasn't so late at night, we could have been caught. But, it was so thrilling. I don't think I'll do it again though."

Jack sighed, "Yes, OK. I'm not sure you're making sense. Be careful. Have you contacted Reissa since you got back? Because I haven't heard from him in quite a while."

"No, not yet. I called yesterday, but he wasn't home. He seems busy. I'll see him soon enough. I'm getting the feeling a lot has changed since I left," she said, and waited.

"Well, yes, for me it has. I'll send you some of the things I'm working on."

Their conversation continued in babbling yin and yang. Snippets of this and that, "huh uh" and "fine just fine." Gabriella slipped a pink tee shirt on and then pulled on black lycra pants; shook her hair to fluff it up.

Still on the phone, Jack said, "You look great." Sunlight filled the room, faded, and returned; voices ethylic and faint.

—◁◁◁ﬀ▷▷▷—

Is it that we might
embrace this day as good?
To appreciate
the magic of our lives
as it unfolds before us?
Bringing gifts of time
and place
and memory
of the comfort of true friends
Are we better people
than we were two years ago?
Maybe so.

*We do cherish each other
don't we?*

We do and always will

—◄◄◄◄◄◄—

"Honey, who was on the phone?" Gabriella asked, arriving with two cups of coffee.

"Just Susanna, she's back from Paris," Jack answered, and added, "Gabriella, I want to tell you about the guides speaking, on the roof a few days ago?"

"Yes, have you heard them again?" she said seriously.

Jack turned to her, held her waist, and said firmly, "That was quite an experience and an awful lot of information. I've decided to transcribe it all from your recorder. I think there is something to it. A message for others. Maybe I can incorporate it in my training sessions. But if I do that or publish it, truthfully, I'm not sure of the rewards."

She held him tight and said, "Listen Honey, I support you. The guides are your own thoughts speaking to you from a larger space. Yes, at times you will say and experience the most esoteric things that may not be well received or reciprocated. Writing about these voices will not be mainstream.

But your training already isn't what I would call mainstream either, and still, you are an excellent trainer; people respect you, and you are a real contributor. What I get is that you are not in the same old basic thing. You add something to it. So, you need to teach others to understand some of the new things you discover and hear. You can do it. You're a natural teacher and enjoy it. I say, go for it."

Gabriella paused before continuing, "I haven't met a teacher yet that does not feel frustrated because they don't get the rewards they expect. There are two things about that. First, teachers commonly don't get the rewards that others, such as business people, expect. Secondly, not being in the mainstream, you are not understood by others until you teach them, and so they don't know what reward goes with what they have learned. Maybe the guides will help you."

Jack turned to face her and said, "Yes, that's what I'm getting."

Gabriella smiled at him, "Well, it's very possible, but this not getting the rewards issue has a circular effect. Because you do reach people who can hear what you're saying. And more and more people are getting it. So as far as rewards go, it hasn't happened yet the way you'd like it to happen, but I'm positive that it will happen at some point. It's probably that you've connected your thoughts to something quite special and not well known; it will take time to unfold. That's just the nature of things and it occurs the way it does. Jack, I've said it before, I believe there's something real that's happening to you about those voices you hear. It's time to take them seriously and share it with others."

She looked him in the eye, "You know this anyway. The human spirit is what interests you. The philosophies of life and all the questions that you've pondered about mankind are what drive you. That's what makes you who you are. You have a lot to teach others and you'll be a success. Sometimes success doesn't have a monetary value. It can just be feeling complete within yourself about what you do and what you contribute to others. Jack, you're on the right track with everything in your life. Trust the voices."

Jack nodded his head affirmatively, "Thanks darling."

WE DO AND ALWAYS WILL

"If we don't touch our heart, our advice to others is heard as noise. No matter what, it is noise delicious and confusing tainted egoium. Screeching through the slippery love calls and yimmy whispers. Waking us with a tap tap on our back late at night to end in silence and a bruised bone." The male voice spoke to Jack as he went on his morning walk.

*Unless requested,
our advice is noise
a snippy exhortation
beneath a weighted hand
beneath a psychic incompetency
beneath our lack of listen
a creaky noise strains
and wails of insecurity
wrought by what is missed*

*return to blood
return to motor
return to simple pulsing moment
gone but in miracle returned
and in miracle so easily forgotten
even with the noise loud
it is barely noticed*

Gabriella woke up late at her place, laid in bed, and wondered how she arrived at this moment. She clicked the TV on to dull the noisy answer to that thought. She waited as morning huddled in a gray and timeless yearn. Yearning for travel to a place of perfection, love, painless love, and vibrant health. Warm and peaceful by the river. Not the doctor's office where today she had an appointment to have a lump in her left breast checked.

She found the telephone, called a client to cancel an appointment, walked slowly to the kitchen, and boiled water for tea.

THE RED CEILING

―⁓ᴜᴜᴜₗʃᴜᴜᴜₗᴏ―

"The Doctor says it's a cyst and wants to remove it," Gabriella explained to Jack.

"Will it leave a scar?"

"Yes, a small one I guess," she said quietly.

They left Jack's apartment and headed up Broadway for Saturday brunch. They found a Turkish restaurant on the second floor at 85th Street. Around the walls were curved booths, intimate and warm; the ceiling was red and the walls a rich saffron yellow. The mood quiet and mid-eastern, the food continental. They sat and ate for hours, and the day washed away. Gabriella loved the color of the ceiling. It gave her an idea to paint her living room. Jack offered to paint it for her.

―⁓ᴜᴜᴜₗʃᴜᴜᴜₗᴏ―

Later that week, Jack went over to paint Gabriella's living room ceiling a cranberry red. It took two days. A two-day gale was predicted, but the storm never came. The ceiling was painted a rich red and the walls a milkypink silk, softer in a turn of brush; the line precise to separate the colors. The result was deep sebaceous warmth in a cave of rest and taste and tallow. They painted, and drank warm sake with dinner – rapini sautéed in butter and garlic mixed with fusilli pasta and served in white ceramic bowls with blue carp in a flip painted on the sides. Gabriella felt the small lump in her breast. She let Jack know how much she appreciates his generosity. Worried about the operation and trying to put it out of her mind, she smiled meekly at Jack.

—◄▥▮▯▮▥►—

Two weeks later, Gabriella went to the surgeon with Jack. When they got home, she showed Jack the incision across the top of her left breast, purple pink and like a smile gone silly. A bruise still yellow with sallow hints surrounds black stitches. She wondered if she'd lost her beauty, if not by hurt, at least by token. It brought to surface evidence of a bad and jimmied irk, and cast suspicion on the whole of her body as if more is hidden under what is red with luck and pink with promise. Bruised and slippery like turmeric and curry spice.

Jack looked into her eyes, less wounded with shine, and bent his head to kiss her wound. Looking up into her eyes, he said, "you're beautiful." Gabriella looked in his eyes, her eyes filled with tears, and whispered, "Thanks."

TWIXT & TWEEN

Susanna:

Glad to hear you're home. Also, heard you'd found another guy. I'm seeing someone also and it's very nice. We have dated about five times. Today I find myself waking up on Sunday to a sunny day in Gotham. Noticeably quiet at 8:30am. How does the world look to you?

I'm in one of those strange states, disoriented to an extent. It's been that way for a week or so. Although feeling a little better today. Yesterday's disorientation was about time. The day flew past, hours leaped and the whole day felt like one-hour. I think this means I'm sensing things at a much slower pace; and time, moving as it does, feels much faster.

I'm in a real betwixt moment in my history. Betwixt jobs, happenings, seminars, friends, and family. It's a "tweener" time for me. If I can calm myself down, it's a good time to write, even though I don't feel I have anything to say.

That usually is when I actually say something worth saying, right?

My twixt and tween times are ones where I practice nothingness and action at the same time. Because I don't know what's next and must cover all bases (to the extent I am willing to use a sports metaphor). I practice nothingness with an outrageous "trusting of the Universe" attitude mixed with following my instincts to eat, sleep, sun on the roof, read, talk and walkabout just as they arrive. I practice action by making cold sales calls, eating ground raw flax seeds with my cereal, and being prudent with my money. All this until I state firmly where I want to be and take aim.

If I can tell anyone anything about life, I'd tell you life is all about "direction." It hardly matters what direction you take, although choosing one that seems interesting or "important" is probably better. Direction may look like going only one way, but seems to always result in going every way. That is, it expands what your life is about. No direction, no development in any part of your life, inner or outer.

So, there is this lull that is formulating my existence. Life seems to spike the moment I chose a direction, or something chooses a direction.

This disorienting lull, twixting & tweening. I admit, I don't know which direction to go.

Let's meet for lunch in the West Village. At that small bakery on the corner of Bleeker Street and West 11th.

Reissa

VULNERABILITY

⸺⧉⸺

Gabriella came over to Jack's apartment. When she entered, Jack was huddled over his computer typing. He turned, waved, smiled, and put his fingers to his lips to signal quiet; then returned to typing. Gabriella walked behind him, rubbed his back, and read over his shoulder for a moment before saying softly, "Vulnerability. I like that. I'll make some tea." Jack continued to write, pausing once in a while to listen.

⸺⧉⸺

"When we open up to vulnerability, we gain power because we are more truthful. However, this is not how vulnerability is usually interpreted. Vulnerability is commonly understood as exposing a personal weakness and, in a sense, this is true. We feel weak because our true nature may be revealed in a manner we are not used to, or that we may expose a false strength and may find we are not what we have pretended to be. These feelings of weakness need not be permanent. Instead, we might build on what is true and in a humble way see our smaller yet potent relationship to greater and greater

truth. In this way, weakness becomes appropriate meekness.

"Weakness is vulnerability guided by irresponsibility and self-doubt. Whereas, meekness is vulnerability guided by responsibility and self-knowledge. The confusion is in the nature of vulnerability, which is a conscious energy that penetrates to the core of our being with a subtle but steady force. When we are meek, we recognize with this energy the appropriate lesser place that ego and identity have in relation to self and essence.

"When vulnerability is distinguished as meekness, it allows access to a common and communal consciousness, which is humanity's greatest power. Vulnerability reveals that we are always whole, and yet always a part of a greater whole. This revelation back and forth from part to whole, and whole to part is ongoing and endless.

"Restricting vulnerability restricts man's true nature and suppresses the innate direction of humanity to explore and create. When we understand the need for vulnerability, we have the key to greater consciousness.

"To open to vulnerability is to be clear about what is most valuable about us. "Usually, in the course of a lifetime of not understanding what is valuable to us, we are left with what feels like a break in belonging, a disconnection in being included by others, and ultimately a disconnection from Source (or Spirit). We are left feeling damaged as if there is something wrong with us, something about us that does not work *correctly. Yet, nothing is wrong. We simply do not understand ourselves. As strange as it may seem, not understanding ourselves is part of the design of being language inventors. It is the discovery of ourselves, which drives our explorations and brings us joy."*

Gabriella was standing behind him. "Yes, that's good. I believe it's correct," she said to Jack. "Who's speaking now?"

"The woman."

"This scenario is played over and over with each one of us, and in this way each person is a holographic image of all humanity. When the ability to use language arrives, our sense of personal value is no longer the same. It shifts and increases to include the power of exploration and creation. This is a new dimension of consciousness, a new whole to live in. Intrinsic to this shift in becoming language users is becoming language inventors, which includes the responsibility for creating representational worlds, worlds that have never existed before. Language transforms potential into practice. This transformation begins when we are very young and continues throughout our lifetime. Suffering is connected to resisting this transformation.

"Language capability and the causation of consciousness exist in us not unlike an incubating egg. This egg is fed by external impressions and early vocable forays. At full incubation, language breaks through its shell and emerges. And, like the young chick, language can

also be very young. Its growth remains dependent upon interaction throughout its life. At the initial manifestation of language, we are left speechless. Eventually, we will be left unfulfilled unless we learn to use language and master it responsibly.

"Our incomplete interpretation of vulnerability is derived from this initial incompetency with language. It is traumatic to experience the power of knowing and the realization of not-knowing ushered in by language.

"This is not how life occurred for us at first. Life was total and complete working on the axioms of pleasure and pain, like and dislike; it was a simple sensate existence with a twist, an incubating egg of knowledge. Only when language is fully manifested do we realize anything, and knowing becomes available. Language, therefore, is the key to noetic capacity. The pre-noetic life is thought without reason. It realizes nothing and exists without the ability or need to understand. It is an enormous shift to go from the pre-noetic to the noetic life. It is going from living in non-doing, unaware of causality to suddenly being responsible for the existence of meaning.

"All anger stems from the shift from pre-noetic to noetic, and the initial trauma of language incompetency in the face of its full revelation. Anger is always a tantrum; an absolute demand to be irresponsible. Ultimately, anger is an unwillingness to be responsible about language, and the impact of each conversation on others. What we seek is to be accepted for who we are, and to be connected

to the source of our power. This power becomes available to us with language. Language opens our ability to play, create, and invent in the noetic and subtle realms of consciousness.

"Prior to language, all is a simple undistinguished determined potential. There is no sense of knowing or not-knowing. No order or chaos. These concepts are collapsed into a single determination with no intent except to live. It is language that has at its core the responsibility to create what is known and to be aware of not-knowing. Language is the means to create something from all that has never been spoken or spoken about. What is at stake is what we truly seek. What we seek to know and create is ourselves.

"Enjoying the capacity to explore, create, and be At-Source for what is known, and doing so with others, is what is essentially extraordinary about humanity."

The female voice vanished.

———◆———

Jack wrote down the conversation, sat for a minute, and read what he'd heard. Then got up and went into the kitchen to have tea with Gabriella.

"What did she say?" Gabriella asked.

He looked up and held his chin thoughtfully in his hand while admiring her deep brown eyes and answered, "I think I have the beginning of a book here." And he handed her what he had written.

CANARY ISLAND BREEZE

Reissa and Susanna met for coffee and cake at the Magnolia Bakery on the corner of Bleeker Street. Susanna kissed Reissa when they met – warm, quick, soft and willow rent. It's midweek and midday, not many people around. They sat on a green plank bench outside across from a women's boutique with large display windows. The lush vanilla cake just freshly baked and still warm, the trees had full leaves and ...

A soft wind blew
from the Southeast from far away
from North West Africa
across the Atlantic
through the Canary Islands
skirting over the Sargasso Sea
and after wafting over Bermuda
lilted hungrily
into New York Bay

The breeze sillied up the avenues, ferreted into the side streets, and blew a scrap of newspaper by Reissa's legs and over his loafers and tickled like Molly's curly hair.

She held her coffee carefully, as an easy steam rose with a twist and headed north with the breeze. The cake intimate and insane with icing sat tidily in a pink paper napkin.

"It's been a while. When you left, everything changed," Reissa winked and took a sip and a nibble.

"We can't stay in old patterns that don't really exist anymore," Susanna answered with a shy bend of her chin and then bit off a small piece of cake. A lip of icing graced her mouth and stayed a minute 'til she licked it gently away. Green fan-leaves fluttered on the Ginkgo trees, and a small brown piece of paper suddenly hurried past, along the curb and towards Chelsea. She notices Reissa sip his coffee and watch the paper scurry off. "So, you're dating. What's her name?"

"Molly."

"Jack knew someone named Molly. He was very interested; she wasn't. I think he scared her off. But eventually he found Gabriella. They're doing very well together," Susanna smiled at Reissa. Her slender legs peeking from draperies. She angles towards Reissa and leans foward. Looking straight at him, chin in hand. "You think it could be the same Molly?"

"It is." He announced triumphantly. He noticed Susanna's eyebrows raised. "She turned out to be my hairdresser one day. I had no idea. We hit it off. I know what you're thinking but, honestly, it was serendipitous. Jack would understand and might even be happy for me." Pausing, he added, "So who are you seeing?" He looked over, admiringly studying Susanna's short red skirt under her long black coat. "You weren't sure if it was warm or cold?" he asked.

"The coat, yes, well I'm fine. Spring's unpredictable these days; anything can happen. Anyway, no, I'm not seeing anyone right now. Just a guy I met on the plane, but he's gone." She paused, "So Jack doesn't know about you and Molly, eh? Ah, don't worry about it. He might be surprised, but he has other things on his mind. It looks very serious with Gabriella."

Reissa stopped drinking his coffee, "Now, I'm the one surprised about that. I don't know how it happened between them. Seemed odd at first, but you're right. It's working out. She seems to bring out the best in him. She understands something about him that goes right over my head."

"Oh please, don't tell me you're jealous," she looked at Reissa and shook her head.

"No. I don't know. Maybe at first. Jack seems to get everywhere and get things that, well, he shouldn't. I mean, how does he know certain things?"

"You'll have to ask him. I think it's what he calls his guides. But, like I'm sure I told you before, and you know this as well as I do, Jack is different. He has a different path. It isn't any easier for him than you or I. Let's remember, we, both of us, left him because we aren't the best people to listen to him, believe him, or support him. I enjoy him as a friend and wish him the best. By the way, I hear he's writing a book with Gabriella." Susanna cocked her head to see his expression.

"Yes, I know. Apparently, as you said, he hears voices, and now he's writing and interpreting what they say. Gabriella encourages him. The gospel according to Jack."

"Now, there it is again; that's a little snarky. Even though, I admit, this is a leap even for Jack."

"Actually, Susanna. I hate to admit it. But, I think he may have something from what he's shown me." There was silence for a moment. They turned towards each other and smiled.

In a wink
In a blink

They looked across the street as they drank their coffee and ate their cakes. The wind had died down. Hush.

With a deep breath and exhalation, Susanna turned to Reissa and said, "So buddy, where are we going? I mean, with our lives." She suddenly looks up. Hey, look at that." She pointed across the street at three light-brown doves flying up to a rooftop. They watched the birds fly in a gentle arc that seemed so fragile. Just as gracefully, they landed on a windowsill in the shade.

After a while, she continued, "I meant, Jack's doing well writing and consulting. He has Gabriella, who apparently is making a go of practicing energy work and therapeutic massage. You now have someone, but are "in-between" work, and I'm ...," she laughed, "independently wealthy, sort of. I've been offered a curator job at the Museum of Modern Art that I'm going to take." She paused and touched Reissa's hair, "Molly – what did you say she does for a living?"

Reissa chuckled, "She's a hairdresser. Really, quite good. That's how we met. I went in one day and she was the one who cut my hair. It was a coincidence."

"There you go," She teased his hair around her right index finger. "Nice. I couldn't do that for you, Reissa."

"Do what, be coincidental or cut my hair?" Reissa asked.

"Cut your hair coincidentally," she joked.

"Ah Hah!! I love you Suzy-Anne, but you're right about that." Reissa laughed and took another bite of cake followed by a gulp of coffee. The wind came up and shifted to the south, shuffling Susanna's coat. A cloud moved and the sun seemed to follow; both moved across the sky, eventually to expire gently and with a wish.

"Like I said, where do we go from here, Reissa?" Susanna stretched and yawned.

Reissa turned to her and held her right hand, "I don't know Susanna. The thing is, I do take some things from Jack. Like he says, and as far as I see it, life's an invitation. The Universe just wants to play. All the time it offers an invitation to play. You accept the invitations and see what's appropriate. Life's always speaking, always inviting. There are messages everywhere. Sometimes encoded, sometimes it's in your face like a billboard; but they're always there if we take time to look and listen. It occurs to me that success may be all about how much we pay attention. How good we are at hearing the invitations.

The thing is, at least to me, following an invitation is important, but secondary. Life fakes us out;

it makes following look like what it's all about. But I don't think so. I think success; I mean joy, happiness, and effectiveness, are more about seeing the invitation clearly and accepting it right up front. What you do with it is secondary. Life is just a game. But getting its invitations at all, that alone really sets the direction of our lives." He turned on the bench and held her hand. Leaning over gently, he kissed her, first on the right cheek and then lightly on her lips. He whispered, "invitations can last a brief moment or they can last forever."

Susanna pulled closer, nuzzled her nose against his. The bark-stewed smell of coffee and sweet cake felt good. "Yes Reissa, I agree. In each moment, invitations arrive. Those moments may be brief or last forever, but are only available if we are first open to the invitation."

They stayed sitting, quietly, sitting. Time slipped by and the sun went west. The ginkgo leaves flickered lime green in the occasional breeze and the late spring light laid purposefully in shimmering streams. As the day progressed, the concrete sidewalk shifted color from powder bright to dusty sand. The black tar road turned from shine to sad. The street was quiet and lazy. They watched when, across the street, a couple in their twenties happened by, the man's arm around her waist. They both were attractive, tall, educated looking, slender, and capable. He was about six feet tall, and she about five feet seven. Her strawberry blond hair giggled straight down the back of her white blouse to her long yellow skirt and white leather loafers. He had dark brown hair, almost black, cut nicely short and styled preppy, horn-rimmed glasses, blue cotton Brooks Brothers button up shirt, off-white khakis, and as Susanna noticed, "burgundy loafers." They stopped to look into the clothing store window at the dresses and perfumes. She pointed and they laughed. She pulled him playfully and they walked away with a bop, bob and bibble. Reissa reached over and grasped Susanna's hand. Susanna rose and with an easy tug pulled Reissa up to her and kissed him long and full on the lips. They both laughed softly.

Still holding hands, they skipped off down the street towards Seventh Avenue and eventually disappeared.

THE UNFATHOMABILITY
OF LOVE

Life gurgles on a request
springing forth from inquiry

Life triumphs when
we touch our hearts,
and ask
our whys, and whats, and wherefores
without expectation
but, with joy and courage
that comes from an urge
to speak honestly

This is a simple quest
met best by exhalation

AFTERWORD

SYMNOESIS

It was summer and Jack was in Maine, staying at Truman Goines' house for a few days. The house was located in a peaceful area outside of Portland; the road ended in a cul-de-sac. Truman lived a bit inland near Steep Falls, along the Saco River in a sparsely built up, small, inserted-1980s development in the woods. Some people turned out to be the solitudinous-Maine-in-the-woods Boston-New York escapees. Not the normal Maine-friendly folk, as Jack discovered.

Truman's home was a generous and comfortable white clapboard house, set back off the road. In the parlor was a wood burning stove with comfy chairs facing it; and Truman's old sunburst Guild guitar leaned against the wall. He had played a song, one they sang back when they first met in their Nudiustertian folk band curiously named, "Yo' Mama's Belly." Truman sang and played his Guild six-string and honked on a beat up Hohner harmonica. Jack played an old Kay stand-up bass (Truman swears he found in a garbage heap in Hartford, Connecticut), chortled in the background, and played various noisemakers, including a large brass gong they'd borrowed from the University music school. They sang an old Noah Lewis song.

I'm gone to German
I'll be back some old day
I'm gone to Ger... man ...
I'll be back some old day
I sail the Newport News ...
somewhere you won't find me

Jack had driven up from New York City and Truman wasn't home when he arrived. His beagle, Elvis, was home and Jack let him out, and then put him back in the house. He decided to walk out to the end of the cul-de-sac to practice his Tai Chi. It was a brisk pine-forest- savory early fall day, and no one was around. Truman and his wife were expected home in about an hour He was alone and the few houses surrounding the cul-de-sac seemed quiet, so Jack assumed the neighbors were still at work or not home. About half way through his Tai Chi dance, a black and white police car rolled down the road towards him, and stopped next to him. The policeman inside the vehicle rolled down his window; he was about 45, possibly ex-military, a bit of short grey hair. Jack noticed his silver badge in the shape of a four-pointed star; in black print was, "Captain Joe L.

Proper, Steep Falls Police Dept." The Captain sat there with an odd look on his face as a rush of warm heated air blew into Jack's face. When the policeman felt he had Jack's attention, he asked Jack a question as if he might be talking to a real jerk, "What ya' doing? I got a call that someone was acting strangely out here."

Jack apologized, "Sorry officer, I'm only exercising. Didn't mean to disturb."

"You sure?" said the policeman. "I don't want to take you in. You can't do that out here. Where ya' from?"

"I'm from New York and visiting my friend, Mr. Goines, who lives right over there." Jack pointed to Truman's house across the street. "I'm sorry I disturbed anyone. That was not my intention."

"Listen, people around here get suspicious of people they don't know, particularly people dancing in the streets. I tend to agree with that. Don't do it again." He stared at Jack for a few uncomfortable seconds. And with that, he rolled up his window and turned around in the cul-de-sac. He stopped, but kept the car running. Jack, a bit startled – not something you would expect all the way out here – figured he better walk towards Truman's house. When he got there, the policeman slowly drove down the road, glanced at Jack, and went out to the main road and disappeared.

When Truman got home, he was as surprised as Jack about the incident. "Sorry about that. We have some older retired people around here who probably got spooked. I'll talk with them."

It was pleasant, with no rain, and each day they walked through the pine woods across from the house. A path led about a quarter mile to a small lake in the full woods. The water was cool and fresh, the trees grew right against the shore, And, there was a small wooded island about 300 yards away. The dog knew the way by heart. It was a late summer afternoon and Maine was perfect – cool air, moist ground, lazy sunlight, with a tang of humus. They walked along, laughing at jokes.

"Why's my hand like a lemon pie? Truman growled in his best Southern drawl.

"I don't know. Why?"

"Caaz, I got's *me-rang-on*."

"Dat's right. Dat's right," Jack chuckled.

They laughed together and talked about many things. They talked about meeting 35 years ago in the ice cream line at the University of Hartford. Truman talked about playing folk music and meeting his wife. His two boys have grown up; one's going to college, the other's starting a lumberjack business and raising his own Malamutes, which he sold. A self reliant man.

Later that week they went to Popham Beach wher they met a year ago. They walked on the beach towards Fox Island, the waves running up, splashing cold water over their feet. The sand was warm. A seagull called. Jack recalled what he had told Truman earlier that summer.

He'd told Truman how he had gone to sit on his apartment building roof, seventeen floors up above Manhattan. As the sun was setting, once again, the guides began talking to him. Since more than one voice spoke to him, he called them "The Committee." The familiar older male voice spoke first. Truman listened.

"Jack, we want to talk about power, partnerships as a new design for human beings, and the language that can create this reality."

There was silence for almost five minutes and Jack didn't know if anything would happen. Then, the voice spoke again.

"Power is spoken desire in action. It is not something forced. It is our word realized. What do we desire? Remember, as an individual we can accomplish only so much. Actually, we are never an individual; we are a community with an identity or series of identities. Identities are roles we design to express ourselves.

If we are truthful, we notice that as an individual we can hardly do anything. Even getting up in the morning and brushing our teeth is a chore. Even that, we do because of our communities, our relationships, partnerships, and promises to others. Think about this. Our individuality is a focusing device, but everything that occurs to us, both positive and negative, and that produces results and lives, occurs in communities, with others in some form of partnership. As an individual, we can hardly accomplish a thing, but as a community, we can accomplish anything. Seek the best partnerships, ones that call you into being and cherish you.

"Community is a network of agreements, language, and conversations. We live in a network of agreements. They are managed by our speaking and listening."

The familiar female alto voice then spoke.

"The Universe is a network of agreements, as a conversation of being. Agreements are the fabric of the Universe. They create and manage the conversations of reality. Understanding and creating agreements is mastering life. Agreements, when they are managed and maintained, will look like partnerships with others and other things. Everything is by virtue of agreement. Everything is in partnership. Disagreement is simple – an undelivered agreement and unfulfilled partnership. Integrity and power occur as agreements are managed and fulfilled. It is a matter of being willing. Being willing to be in partnership. Being willing to be powerful and to empower others.

"Let me speak to you about mastery," she paused. *"One of the capacities of an adult human being, a true master, is a powerful relationship with not-knowing, with a beginner's mind. In other words, to be an adult is to put ourselves in front of not-knowing. Therefore, trust is about our relationship to the unknown. In the present, to see reality as it is, and to speak is the ultimate power. For many people, reality is highly underrated.*

"If we go beyond the place where we normally quit, where we sense a boundary and we stop. When we take one step beyond that, we are accessing mastery. We do not do this alone. All problems are solved by partnerships. We must manage the network of agreements that manage the network of agreements. A master is a manager of this network. I know I have said this before, but it is the essence of partnerships. We are empowered by everything everyone says and does. Be powerful."

The deeper male voice spoke.

"I want to talk to you about partnering." A western breeze blew by and a piece of paper scurried about the two foot high edges of the roof. *"Partnerships are the foundation of our lives. They are experienced day-to-day as empowering each other in an exploration of ongoing growth and development. In partnership, we identify agreements, manage those agreements, commit our resources to fulfilling the agreements, and are accountable for the agreements and their outcomes. Partnership is not the managing of competing*

monologues. Partnership is managing dialogue; the network of agreements that gives reality." He paused. *"There is no greater dialogue, nothing more effective than a promise – a managed dialogue that causes the present to occur. It is the most powerful creator of reality. A promise sustains and gives ultimate purpose to partnership. It is how our world is realized. Other than our gratitude expressed as a simple "thank you," a promise is an expression of power. It is access to the power and practice of partnerships.*

"Partnering represents the interdependence and integralness of all things. Dialogue is essentially participating and creating in not-knowing, as it occurs only in the present. What we get, is ourselves. Surrender monologue to the dialogue. Be willing. Only dialogue exists. Monologue is an illusion.

There was a long silence.

"Further, we cannot emphasize this enough: Language is the property of community, not individuals. We are in relationship with each other because of dialogue, the in-between, the invented in-between. Again, the easiest, clearest way to presence dialogue is to say, 'Thank you' for small and large things. To be human is to be a partner, to be more than. We have surrendered to 'I'. Now, we can surrender to 'We,' the empowered 'We,' and say thank you; and all will be present." Being aware, mastering the language, standing in mystery, surrendering to We, actualizes true power."*

After a moment, the first voice came back.

"We live in a world of our own design with others who also live that way. There is no circumstance or facticity that designs our lives. Everything is a product of our own design. Even our birth. Whatever we cause, that's what we live in. We are the masters of our life. What are we going to do with it?

"Most people speak a language of default. That is, they don't think. They say what other people say before them. That is from the past. Not from the now, and certainly not from the future. We are creating a language that reinvents "human being". What if we could start from a different point than "I"? If we change the language, everything changes. If we start from partnership, we would already be partners; a language of the integral. We would already have trust in the field of partnership. We would already have abundance. We would never be alone. We start from, we don't have to get to, partnerships We are already there. Beyond right way and wrong way. Beyond trust and judgment. We begin in a new field of human potential. I'll meet you there."

~···~

Your love guides me
through life
Of all people
You are at the top
Thanks for coming to planet Earth

THERE'S AN ABUNDANCE OF YOU

There is an abundance of you

There is a screaming hunt
and filled gushing share
that holds the veil of bone
and hand
and joy
that is at times
a fine and sheer transom
above the starved and reaching delicate arm
an arm that is not so strong
or brave
or steady
no one to gather shattered pieces
or sweep the floor

There is a large and moving silence
warm and heated tropics hush
a weighted stingy poor request

for finger touch
as was the last listened gentle return

It's held so well
your hidden loss and loneliness
your teething, grabbing shop-bite tears, and
panicked wanting knowing
wanting breath on and for breath
always there before you
and never quite in hand

What need is there for hands like this?
so feeble
such poverty in grip

It's strange
how there is no request
no gathering
of breath and sweaty nape
of nap and muscled back, or
upper leg or calf
no gathered wedded leaf, or grain or fruit
no strength to take, but
will to leave it be

And, only when a new west
wind arrived with Spring
and only as the sun set
and only when you rested with a head so
strained and crying
was a hint of need, or

was it want or wish?
and that, as this as air

As temporary
as an elf-sneeze wink
and yet, I cannot move!
I cannot let go!
that juggle-tense
and earnest worried shallow
worried weight
and worry

Less able than I thought
less practiced
in affect and giving

That worry as an opening
for waff
and whiff
and drift

⚊⚊⚊

There is an abundance of you

I'm not ready to speak
not ready to share something intimate
I hardly know you

I hardly know you
just met you

What missed report, or
raging gaping
would you see
in my moments of joy
or weep?
What trembling lip and cheek
what wavering casual nod would you detect
in my real life?

That story is so real
real
and so known
by touch and memory of touch
and staring gaze
as sunlight on your gold-brown hair
away you walk out on the shore
to swim
as sunlit naked
as shaped and light
as memory
and sheepish backward glance
and grin

What listening is there for memory
and world worn past
and long past draping youth
and now that passed and passed
with age and
full of time
that now I'm ld
and not with you
I've never seen a memory so young

and full of shimmer and
bold imagination
of your toothy grin
full of tease
joy-felt eyes

There is a touch of body memory, and memory
felt deep muscle know, and know
and indescribable
undistinguished from me
Is it felt or known
or part of tissue, blood and bone?
This thought I see
is deep within
and caused and shapes my every step
and every word
there is no demarcation
between step
and felt
and thought
or, water on your shoulder
curved and
grooved straight back
hair hung
flash and bright ripped auburn hair
a gentle curtain past your neck
and stated about your back

What good is this old memory and yarn?

I'm just not ready to speak
to share
not ready to be intimate

I hardly know you

—◁◁◁◁⟨∫⟩▷▷▷▷—

There is an abundance of you

There is an abundance of you
fears that challenge
bind and drag
and pinch
in the night
are
doors
to power, love and joy
Yet, courage
and fear
are managed
and the stand
we take
in the matter
of our own created existence
is choice

And choice
begins with responsibility
a choice
of how
we will cause

our every existence
in fear, or
in love with generosity
or flight
a simple
never ending choice

—⸨⸩—

There is an abundance of you

It's a pity
that the days can be so short

day and day link together
with each forgotten separate moment
they rust, fade
the touch by touch is lost
great gaps
in where we've been

And yet, one link
one solid look of face
and chin and lip met eyes
pungent and as blossoming
as striking as a hand held face
and palm felt cheek
and thumbs to mouth
and lightly touch to eyelid
kiss
is full of saturated salt

and need
and stare

There is a gentle fullness in that gracious face
and wide and soft beam eyes
dark and grey and brown
there is fullness to those arching cheeks
and grasping lips
met with the rising sun

And, rising face and nose to cheek
and breath to breath
and lash of eye to eye lash, and
gentle grip of hand
face held
cradled and caressed and cooed
and kept in hand
hair and nape of neck
on palm of hand
balanced and benign and beaming

There are deep plowed fields in those eyes
fellows working sweat
and women wading knees bent
long hot weather
haze and bright sun
greens and wheat
and might red horizons
laid and swooped
to hold a body full of warmth
soft and leg strong

close and back unbent
palms and look held high

There is a bite
and sure bite
a tight and rooted grip
grip and laid grip ponder
ponder pounce
and ripple of last jawing
jaw and wind
and pressing swirl of body close
is body wandered close
and vital
in that Spring
and earth rolled peat
and tug

There is the round and soft
of sun light dazzling
up from throat
and flowing from that full and useful face
that never ends
that is a gaze eternal
in a forward look
a human found and earth found beam and
seek and wonder
a spreading lip met tooth teeth grin
safe and stretched with eye
a smile
no offense
no quick to pounce
or bite in deed

an offering of wealth, and
welcome body close
and snug and rum
less a snarl
more a nibble close, and
safe joy wanting

What great joy
and tonic joy
is there in such a speechless flowered look?
look held light with grin and fancy
thought and thanks
stolen with such ease
with such full and linkless charm
its charmful
charmless
charmlink
kiss

⟨⟨⟨⟩⟩⟩

There is an abundance of you
There is

There is an abundance of you
tan dark hair
slight and bending
with nothing on
wrench in hand
tightening loose bolts
on the new faucet
just installed in the tub

304

There is an abundance of you
a sincere and straight intention
a work that fits
and is a back-bent curve
neck and eyes on purpose
steel wrench and balanced hips
and hair it hangs so long
charged with evening brown
a wrap of darkest night
fall straight to ground
ripples with each twist of wrench
just in time to bathe

There is a dawn light
that powers through a small bathroom window
closed and snug and fighting dawn
there is a fighting chance
and choice to fight
from power or fatigue
fight and whisper full of shame
and full of trepidation
full of declaration
tears that overflow with simple generosity
a shame of missed acknowledgement
and, drunken mixing guilt, and guilt
lame and past and beat

There is an ever generating
present passion
often lost between the twist and wrenching turn
beneath a robe of many colors
many weaves

and swift and not so swift escapes
that battle cotton
into a firm and special armor
yet weaker than the breath within
that teases through dry winded lips
and utter sweet that tear
precious wet
and precious flown and fluttered
precious greet

There is a deep and quiet space
a quiet deep and present
skin-wrapped space
that is as safe
and open with a kiss
as fragile skin
is skin held mystery
tight and tooled as wrench held tight
and twist and wrench shared
naked
bath shared
twist of greet and hair swept mighty
mighty circled triumphant arms
great broad and body greet
in bathtub filled
and bathtub broad, and
deep with work
wet work
work shared wet
and wet-shared

There is an abundance of you

There is a wall
a line of trepid demarcation
that separates destiny from desire
known and
an unknown capability from courage
as apple from tree
a night like no other night

Where there is scarcity
where things are scarce
there is a wall
huge and tall and fog-filled
And where there is abundance
where things are abundant
there is choice
complete
to flatten wall to line
to burn off fog
and call the belly, chest and throat
to a hearty ownership

Scarcity is incomplete
but in abundance
completeness is declared
and is as much as it is
deep and rich-dark

Scarcity holds fragmentation
fall to knees bewildered

an attachment to so many
separate pieces

Abundance declares completeness
commitment
stated full and whole
as true as true and what is not
a roar of destiny
a leap of wonder
chance
and soar

———

There is an abundance of you

I love to hear your voice
huddled close and
pressing full against my ear
so all the breath and hush
and chomp is there

There is a comfort of sounds
you make
each story
a hint of song
connected with a careful mash
of mouth and tongue and
deep escaping breath chant chest and lung work
deliberate and working generated self

I love to hear your voice
placed out on the listening
that will make it true

I love to see
long shape of swelled sprung apple, pear and
plum placed swan neck
curved swan legs
long and bright and ankle slender
leg and burst of calf and thigh
that is so bare
so held and grip
and angled with delight
terrified with chance
and heart held deep escaping gasp
drawn from an ancient beast
who found a trip of delicacy
and held the light skim blade of shin
a gentle curved bone twig of ankle
high and hap held high
and heard the true escaping self
with foot held
against a slightly tilted cheek
against a firm and subtle plum-touch-thigh
that surges past forgiving rounded knee

There is a sitting crease of hip
and bend of knee
and gilt of tilted angled ankle
tilted with a mild blush of bone
that is frozen in time and grace
a flip of gentle purpose brow

and belly twist and bend
beneath a shaded blink of passing eye

A passing turn
and broken close of time
caught in solid memory
in solid know and print
knowing blended mid-hid calf
as seen and recognizable as name
across a room
as blazing as a hand held torch
in a child's hand

What ankle bone and hip and
collar print and cheek
is close and deep behind deep breath and look?
what is held before my eyes?
light and light-shaped
touch and caught in full
and caught as bare and
light of bone
as full of flight
and full of power-leg-taught-walk
walk across the room
and to the door
and leave

━◅◖〰〰〰◗▻━

There is an abundance of you

Come
Come here
Stand outside before you leave
and let there be a quiet gushing wait
an instant stare
blown breeze
and guess
and charge
Before the night is begged
before the evening tumbles, and
smiles linger
and fade as pungent tossing lives
invented
in this night
disappear

There is a healthy stage point purpose
in your walk
a skip attentive place of toe and hip and turn
and there is a crazy half-thought vague
familiar stated space sought
through a held and real tenderness and giving
the life you left
eroding
with such force and fun and fancy
the life left behind

There is a stage of the possible
arrived with one step
one choice
one brave look and step
all this in the breeze

that came with such intent
a fair look
face swept breeze
hair dark and fluttered back
bright and lifted cheeks
straight and rapid eyes
inquisitive
lips held soft past question
and rounded broken leave

And there now I left
with fool felt turn and drive
nothing said
nothing left to say
I left with one last look, and
stopped a moment later
at a small convenience store
bought a chocolate almond bar
ate it
slowly
heading north
against the sweet Spring breeze

There is an abundance of you

Touch
in the morning
morning
brushing nose and face
and warm well slight roll wallow
that came

with a slight breaking grey
and bluish gray-green dawn
warm and stewing
pensive easy draping
body stretch and fall
ease dropping jelly fall
fall found hips
upon a warm and stir-stewed call
call and rest, and
want gentle willing yawn

Yawn that yaws and fills and lifts
and bends true back to work
holding breathing chest
lost damp fall
heavy morning lost
and falling
lost and lazy rest
a fertile dream
with laden push-pear breasts
strong and shoulder-shaken silence
silent generosity
swelling ancient tender taught-tilled sleep
easy calling met instant wonder
Touch and rounded
settled form found hip and
tender weathered nape of sweat neck
closed eyes
in one last look
sleep and sleep-slurred
far and reaching touch of time and wish
Time turns and powers endless power

effortless in leap of light
and journey leap
wish that shouts and hounds and plays
pure chance and challenged cat, and
rip and fear-flung courage cat-chanced challenge

Touch warm and slack bid belly bid
in molding grace
full body grace
and sourced found full
line found air rushed breath
blood pumped proud
grip torn great
eye fall as less sleep left
eye closed and dropping
draped on full round beam and spark
flow in not a thought
or what rose to stretch
rise yawn
rose yawn
to what gives light
to early sought and wandered wait-washed day

⤛⬗⤜

There is an abundance of you

White high dogwood petals
pop and gem
and luster on a light
and bent up limb
curved and swept and reaching

dance high lifted float
jeweled and stated sneak on twig
found chirp chop popping baubles

Baubles flit and fury flutter
flurred and peppered mightily
sing and rest in morning lull
with petal reach, and
twig bait wink se[?] tongue start

Rabbit run below
twitch and hop quick
turn and daring eye plugged pop
and see among the new fresh greens
a scurried anxious sneak

Dart and swoop of tiny brown bird
carries canvas motion
citing seconds passing
notice inching welling day
rise call by call and
twitch by twitch
and new invented run
invented tag and
purpose pop found grab and grow

Tug a little
hop a little
swoop a gen, and
shop a little

Simple song set bright

behind a funny dash
across the lawn
behind the fenced-in garden
while rumbles in the dawning house
hold bang
tight with silence challenged
hushed when noise is stopped
that silence
ready to reclaim, and
dance with zing precise
with quick and hurried
hungry call

Hunger in a molting pat pull pang
and pit
ring and wait
and sing along

What worry is there in wait like this?
this interrupted silence
This silence interrupted
in full and flowered morning
this force filled push, and
flowered burst bay bin
jumped firm and arching
reaching out
to offer fling flash lure
and invitation
called
lured and draping
swing and swoop
and gift pluck

gentle breath pluck
hold and joy
fit and match, and
taste the spreading beaming shop
while heads rest
cheek pressed warm
against a kneeing wait-knelt
want

Rest and sit
with reach and
gift gave gaze
white dogwood flower sits
held high
held gift
jeweled and light filled
sourced and lighted jewel
share and shine with share
announced before the green and
lifted by a twig
lifted
called and
given freely

─◁◆▷─

There is an abundance of you

Kneel
full
and hair raked down
chin slight tilt

317

soft and pensive eyes look lighted
lifting full and sweet felt full
and body present
skin as burst and plain
and full of rain and dew
and lightly leavened body wheat and rise
and touch-like
truly present in a swoop of line and burst
in gentle teaching chin tilt
Chin and heart curved rap
and deft dealt deep
and separating deep
found heart filled heart
and press

What great giving joy
and passing wish
What withered bothered wonder
passed this way?
and, left in stillness
hand loss
no-known present skin felt
hair light
and burn across swooped back
laid low

There is air
and there is mouth
and empty taste held firm
and know
cooed instant know
beat and joy and ply

filling body sense rip ripe
deep and present sure shocked sure
pout and purred pay
pay taste pound and bite
soft bite

What is where wend whip
and wonder weld and grip?
passed sure pressed sure fruit
found full chest pressed-up greet kneel life
a state and stated plum
and risen knee held shoulder cross so firm
and full of light
light full grip and squeal
silent wishing give
arch bent back give
present sweet and swoon bound give
take lighted beast
and helping held hold hip
hip and hold
lip met eye
and lip sought rip
hair back tilt give arch

Light blue linen dress tugged loose
around your waist
held buzz and baiting
left and shorn sun shock and drop
and there is stated true
unbound beamed and pleasant
stayed and straight nude nothing fill
and nothing lost

and nothing wanted
left unwanted or wondered

There is true love
There is what is left of hope
A lack of fear
a loosened left and lingered fading hope
as far from thought
as that thought longed for
by others

There is found a beast laid bare
a found-beast roared and raw
with fine and fill bend fury
There is a soft and gracious gift as well
on knee and tilt
and chin held gaze
there is a hesitancy lost in grace on knee
and given beast fond
found as given beast

———

There is an abundance of you

Dark
and waiting
hurt and hurried
sing and zip woo holler
hold and beg
for full blue listening "yes"
hold dark sweet

back broad
mellowed swoop of back
and great tease bound give
tease sweet
Flirt
of eye tilt flirt blinked back
eyes mist wet
seen and moist
with light and
feathered mist melt tug
back rise and
head rest prayer
golden bend, hair gasp, and thigh
thigh bold and stated broad done willy-well
worked and harbored loft
and lifted over bayed booed bounty
hurried hope left instantly
in that full and gathered
beamed and bayed horizon

There is a shuttered heart
and breath and air-filled gelt-sourced mutter
bath of misted present sought bound ache
and weathered whiff and wonder
wonder laid worn head
above that thigh
heavy on a drifted soft
and wet mist back

The gathered long and brilliant trek
the ever present walk of man and wife is set
with swooping curve and plunge and dive

through soft back rub
hand upon your shoulder blade give
comfort comes from every step
and distant gaze
and hard set hike and toll
found in our fun and varied touch
and lifted passing close
breath gave warm
and gentle gifted whiff and blaze
gift breath and ginger mist rest mourning dove
and dew
For there is comfort when we stop and rest
if there is two

There is always more than one
and never one that is an only settled rest
and never one that is an only man
left with only hope
And always is that hope a deeper mist before us
poured from our hearts
and emptied with an open eye
the gentle reach of hand is filled
as full
as reach

—⊶⊷—

There is an abundance of you

Tell the light
that races through this sparkling dawn
that full and sigh broke lemon light

how quiet is this early gentle day
how sweet the grazing hush of our awakened
Spring
our subtle touch
our fingers touch
and fingers rippled along my arm and back
roll and hold kept ladened sleep rush hug
holding press warm body sing

I still hold a swim push leap joy charge of love
and I still hear that love sung great
in unexpected found heart full complete
announcing anthem
Sing and stated
chewed chowed cheek give lip
love bound lovers lip
found heard and
given pure and simple self
and given gracious heart
that is as much as me
as much as I am you

And if there is another clear and sunbuilt day
in our hands
there would not be lost
a good and fair tomorrow
passed our lips, or
that good gaze of swallowed
beaming eye-held love and
present in good food
and forest found far found
bee buzzes

and bear that reaches
with great full grasp and hold

Yellow clear and bright
tossed brilliant sourced bound morning
across the grass green leaves
across hushed and murmured pillow
hushed and wink built
make and look-see
eye wink flash wink wet lash
and lift sneak lemon grin
bailed light
hint of powered evening
lingered warm
and lingered tart
and tasty

———

There is an abundance of you

The reassurance of familiar smiles
a smart and lifted chuckle
the time you share with me
the delicate encoded hint of care
and lip press hands held
I hand on every word
that wells and breathes
everything you say brings power
and clears out all the mist
surrounding love

Late night walks
are full of great discovery
what is shared in conversation
discovered in a simple walk evening walk
a turn of foot
a reach of hand
a glance toward faded sunset
red stop-light blinks
on and off
time to touch and
hold you close

Yet, if I never see your smile again
and I am lost in some interpretation
some evading rhythm held
or faded off key song we sang
I'll wait
and make a story of our lives
and say that if you hold it in your hands
as book
It's all there
blither bib and baffle

If I never hear your voice again
and that will surely happen
as conversations disappear
when left to our sheer wanting
I'll walk
and sing a melody of what it was with you
and what was hidden in your sweet
and string give sing

And if I lose your touch
and reach is filled with air
I'll wait again
and place a word out on the wind
and build the warmth and gentle touch
beam bound jet-joy rankled
stare whine and mated moan meld bite

Yet, I have that churn and huckled chuckle
and still I have a deep wish wonder as I wait
for our next say and walk
I still have a word or two
before our every step

Never have I lost a soul
never has a soul been left lost
for there is always steps behind those words
words many
and steps plenty

The End

AUTHOR'S NOTES

This story is based on real occurrences just before the 21st century began. The digital world had emerged and the singularity of man and machine was closing in fast. This had a counter balance; a release. A new chakra above the heart was opening to new capacities. Capacities of being and consciousness. Humanity was evolving and a symnoetic human being was emerging; *'Homonoeticus'*. It could have been the surge of the Millennium responding to this emergence, or it could have been that Jack had reached an abrupt stage in his life that required reconciliation. The question, "Who am I?", hounded him. The world was in flux and so was Jack. It must have felt to Jack that sometimes you come to a cliff and the only thing to do is leap off it. Because when you turned around, there was another cliff behind you, surrounding you. You leapt, that is, you gave everything away literally let go of everything. And, what you found out is that about 90% comes back to you in one form or another. For instance, if you end one relationship another arrives, and the next relationship is always better. That is if you truly leapt in the first place. Anyhow, what returns has much of what you left, but also something new, something different. The difference can be a challenge.

Jack: I think I expected more rewards. Why I'm not sure. There's the disappointment in not getting what I want when I expect it. I know I insist in the most esoteric avant garde modalities at times that are not well received or reciprocal. I'm not often mainstream, but still, I sensed I was, and am, a contributor.

Gabriella: The majority of people are not and that's why there is less rewards at this time - you are not in mainstream so you need to teach others to understand. You're a natural teacher and enjoy it - I haven't met a teacher yet that does not feel frustrated because they don't get the rewards they expected. So it's two things, teacher not getting rewards expected in this society is common and not being in the mainstream you are not understood by others until you teach them. It's almost like a circular effect, but not quite because you do reach people that can hear what you're saying and more and more people are and will be getting it. So as far as rewards go, it hasn't happened yet the way you'd like it to happen - but I'm positive that it will happen at some point. It's just the nature of things that it occurs the way it does. The human spirit is what interests you, the philosophy of life and all its questions that you've pondered on all your life is what drives you. That's what makes you who you are - you have a lot to teach others and you'll be a success. Sometimes success doesn't mean monetary value, it can just be feeling complete within yourself about what you do and what you contribute to humanity. You're on the right track with everything in your life.

Jack: Yes. Thank you. This is what I think.

If we are human beings on a spiritual journey than we are rational actors bounded by our private thoughts, desires, wants, and needs. We can only experience the limitedness of our private monologues and a life spent having them acknowledged. The rational actor manages a neurotic anticipation of becoming. The world does not occur now, it will occur someday, one day, and it did occur someway at some time.

If we are spiritual beings on a human journey than we are transrational actors. We might not be 'beings' at all but aspects of

'Being' unbounded by privacy, as it doesn't truly exist. We experience the actualization of unlimitedness; of collective dialogue that pushes the event horizon of language, inventing new communication and opening up new worlds of reality. We experience this unboundedness in a holographic now. That is; all that is, is manifest now. The transrational actor manages what everything is as *Now*.

Both aspects are intermingled and correct in describing the human experience. The trick is to know which aspect we should lead with and which aspect should be supportive. It is the balance of identity (personality) and essence, in which identity is less than 50% and essence more than 50%. But, each not fully diminished.

The 'Symnoesis' hypothesis notes that human beings consist of two entities: human and Being in a symnoetic alliance. One appears fully dependent upon the other. Not unlike the biological relationship between mitochondria and humanity in which two biological entities have evolved to sustain each other as one organism. This is a hint at our true nature. We are not one entity, but many. We do not have one essential nature; we do not have one mind;

we do not have one requirement; we do not have one appetite. We have a partnership.

In the case of the human + Being partnership, we experience an intertwining of two fully alien entities. So, alien to each other in understanding and ability to perceive that the other can not be understood let alone be encountered. This is the most difficult aspect of this partnership; it is fully and completely hidden from our cognition. It can only be assessed by reflection. When it is assessed the only information we obtain is about ourselves; a reflection of authenticity. In this way, we perceive that the partnership is an exploration in knowing ourselves. This is the spiritual journey obtained through our humanity.

Gabriella: Excellent, my love. I'll see you tonight. Around 7.

SYLPHID DREAMS

—◆—

... fleet thought frittered brain debris
nip the nim bit brittle tip of inquiry
hardened by deduction
... whipped clean of dew
by love's lessened comedy ...

buddy, can you spare a dime?

morning poked its nose around the corner of
dark delicate shadow aestivating troll sniffed
silky molten air spit with mung and mudro calls
the light that breaks the dark "raw" and settled
into a loss of friend though less insistent is more
persistent ...

light
dark

all was dark
but never will
all be light

what moved and shaped the shadow
moved with grind and roar ...

what moved with silence
building shadows depth
with simple delight
sipped the nectar
from the edge of light's retreat ...

nibble old Ecru
taste the dram
with one eternal lick ...

light is not a concept hidden in etuis
but an inquiry of what it's not
neti neti
not spag-etti

Made in the USA
Middletown, DE
10 January 2023